What the critics are saying...

"*Layover* is a great book. *Ms. Hardin* has written a wonderful book with both sides of the story which will make you want that happily ever after for Jack and Kira." ~ *Ann Lee Just Erotic Romance Reviews*

"*Ms. Hardin* has written a story of love and lust set against the backdrop of the airline community that I enjoyed very much. *Layover* is a keeper." ~ *Susan White Just Erotic Romance Reviews*

Ann Wesley
HARDIN

Layover

An Ellora's Cave Romantica Publication

www.ellorascave.com

Layover

ISBN # 1419953125

Edited by: Briana St. James
Cover art by: Syneca

Electronic book Publication: June, 2005
Trade paperback Publication: December, 2005

Warning:

The following material contains graphic sexual content meant for mature readers. *Layover* has been rated *E-rotic* by a minimum of three independent reviewers.

Ellora's Cave Publishing offers three levels of Romantica™ reading entertainment: S (S-ensuous), E (E-rotic), and X (X-treme).

S-e*nsuous* love scenes are explicit and leave nothing to the imagination.

E-*rotic* love scenes are explicit, leave nothing to the imagination, and are high in volume per the overall word count. In addition, some E-rated titles might contain fantasy material that some readers find objectionable, such as bondage, submission, same sex encounters, forced seductions, etc. E-rated titles are the most graphic titles we carry; it is common, for instance, for an author to use words such as "fucking", "cock", "pussy", etc., within their work of literature.

X-*treme* titles differ from E-rated titles only in plot premise and storyline execution. Unlike E-rated titles, stories designated with the letter X tend to contain controversial subject matter not for the faint of heart.

Layover

Dedication

It's been said that writers are born, not made. And there's certainly a great deal of truth to that statement. But it doesn't tell the whole story. Without an enormous, enduring support group, without inspiration from others, and without someone believing in your potential enough to give you a chance, all the talent in the galaxy won't take you very far.

When success happens, there are always so many people to thank. But this, my first published book, is dedicated to the following:

For my awesome editor, Bree, who plucked Layover from obscurity and made a glorious dream come true. You set the course for the rest of my life with one, simple e-mail. How can I adequately thank you?

For the Bats, whose unselfish guidance and considerable intelligence made this book suitable for submission. You're the wind beneath my wings.

For my family, for cheering me on and reminding me often that quitting was not an option. If I can do it, so can you.

But mostly,

For my dad, Frank, and for my brothers, Mike and Rob—my magnificent men in their flying machines. Though your wings have folded, you will soar in my heart forever. Godspeed, my heroes.

Trademarks Acknowledgement

The author acknowledges the trademarked status and trademark owners of the following wordmarks mentioned in this work of fiction:

Cadbury: Cadbury Limited Corporation

BMW: Bayerische Moteren Werke Aktiengesellschaft Corporation

Camaro: General Motors Corporation

Mini Cooper: Rover Group Limited Company

Zero Halliburton: Zero Manufacturing, Inc. Corporation Delaware

Trojan: Church & Dwight Co., Inc .Corporation, Delaware

Chapter One

Moral dilemma number one –
Is it ever okay to want to boink your best friend?

"See? She's just like you." Jack Grayson pointed to the image of the *Runaway Bride* on the TV screen. "The Queen of Disposable Men."

"Will you stop calling me that?" Kira Allen shot back.

"You throw men away." He snapped his fingers. "Like that."

"I do not." At least not most of the time. Or some of the time. Except for maybe once. Okay, twice—that she recalled.

And with good reason. Kira had recently raised her standards. While she'd built her career as an airline copilot, she hadn't minded dating men who were out for a good time. Now, she wanted more. At twenty-eight, she was ready to begin the search for a mate.

"Most of them deserve to be tossed. But still," Jack continued.

Seated next to him on an orange sofa in her condo, Kira stared straight ahead, and wondered why they always ended up bickering, just like they had as kids. She could blame Jack, but truth be told, she enjoyed the one-upmanship that had colored their relationship forever. "And you're better?"

According to Pan Air legend, Jack had a revolving door policy when it came to women in general, flight attendants in particular. He never talked about his love life, but Kira'd never seen him hang with anyone for long, except her, and as his best friend, she didn't count.

Jack shrugged. "We're not talking about me."

"Same old, same old," she muttered. He took the liberty of dissecting her love life at every opportunity. But let her mention his and he clammed up. "Are you afraid for Arlo?" she asked. "Is that it?"

Arlo Jacobs, Quality Assurance Officer and Regular Joe, held current boyfriend status in Kira's life. She had high hopes for this relationship. Arlo seemed settled, serious and *quiet.* He'd shown no signs of wanting to control Kira's world. A far cry from Jack, who was currently making such a pest of himself she wanted to toss him out a window—at thirty-thousand feet.

Except he had his uses.

She hadn't met any decent men during her tenure as copilot for Seaboard Express—a tiny, commuter airline that made daily 'milk runs' up and down the east coast. Except for the rare single businessman and even rarer single pilot, the pickings had been slim enough for her to start to worry. It wasn't as if she was a party gal with weekly opportunities to date. She preferred the solitude of the beach at night to the thrum of a singles bar or comedy club. Despite her quieter nature, however, she *had* managed to snag several dates over the years by reluctantly attending Jack's infamous Pan Air bashes. For a multitude of reasons—namely Jack threatening to peel their dicks like a banana if they misbehaved—those romances never quite worked out.

She sighed.

At least things were looking up. Now she flew for Pan Air International thanks to him. Using his clout as a respected captain, he'd pulled strings, put in a good word. She'd completed the interminable company training course that Arlo helped develop and teach, passed with flying colors and here she was. "You're the one that enabled me and Arlo. You have only yourself to blame."

"Don't remind me." Jack leaned back on the sofa, scraping his face and running strong fingers through wavy dark hair. "I hate him."

"No surprises there." He hated all her boyfriends and didn't seem to notice the role he played in their departure. What would he care if she disposed of them properly when the time came?

"He's a dipshit," Jack said.

Kira rolled her eyes. "He's nice enough."

"For what?"

"My purpose."

"And that would be?"

She couldn't say for certain. Far too early to tell. Arlo didn't make her pulse jump like flying did. Or stimulate her mind the way Jack did. But bodies weren't built to endure that kind of relentless excitement forever. Neither were emotions. Kira had an exciting job so what she needed at home was peace and quiet. At least she thought that's what she needed. "Marriage," she taunted.

As expected, Jack displayed the strangulated symptoms of a man having a coronary. "You can't marry that jerk. He's a wingless nerd who makes life miserable for pilots—you included."

"He's making sure you're fit to fly," she countered mildly. "Keeping the passengers safe."

"You bought that corporate crap?" Jack spewed. "Pan Air has enough quality control built into the system without wasting profits on dickless wonders with wing envy."

He had a point but no way would she admit it. To do so would make Arlo seem redundant. Since she was investigating the possibility of a future with him, she didn't want to go there.

"He sits in the cockpit, clicking his frickin' mechanical pencil and pushing paper up his corporate ass."

Kira placed a hand over her mouth to keep from smiling. If she didn't react, he'd eventually shut up.

Not this time.

He must've sensed he wasn't getting anywhere because he changed tactics. She had to hand it to him. He was quick on his feet.

"Besides the asshole factor, Jacobs puts his life on the line every time he goes to work—flying in problem aircraft with problem pilots. He'd leave my nieces and nephews without a father."

"They wouldn't be your nieces and nephews."

"You always say that. It's your way of disconnecting." Jack punched his thigh. "You want Arlo to be the father of your children?"

Kira tuned him out while he raged. She could marry Arlo and she would, if he met her stringent criteria. After several dates, it looked somewhat promising, but you never knew. She currently harbored considerable doubt in the sex department. So far, Arlo seemed challenged that way—basically because there hadn't been any. Kira had no clue what that was all about. And now more than ever she didn't want to ask Jack for advice. It was way too much fun to sit here and piss him off. "You or I could die too, Jack. One hydraulic failure and it's over, baby." She lifted the lid on the pizza box, considered a fourth slice, and took a swig of warm beer instead.

"But I wouldn't be leaving a family behind."

"Eventually."

"Not getting married." Jack picked the pepperoni off his slice with a disgusted look and threw it onto her empty paper plate. "How can you eat that shit? I want to come and go when I please, no responsibilities, no complications."

Yeah. And most of the time he came and went between her condo and his. "That's such a crock. You spend every free second with me. You hate your so-called freedom." She flicked the pepperoni into her mouth and savored the salty, fatty texture. In the world according to Jack, she'd be in a coffin by forty if she continued eating so haphazardly. She'd done everything right so far. Why not live a little now?

"That's because I haven't had any yet," he said.

"What's that supposed to mean?"

An accusatory look entered his eyes and pinned itself to her forehead. "With Mike in Colorado and your dad—" he cleared his throat, "dead, who else is going to look after you?"

"*Look after me*?" A slurry of love mixed with irritation sloshed around in her stomach. Tom Allen, her father, had guided his children and Jack on one principle and one principle only—if you screwed up, you died.

A war veteran and bomber pilot, he knew what could happen if you lost control of a situation. This battlefield philosophy had invaded every fissure of his being, and though he'd lovingly and patiently gifted Kira with the drive to succeed, he'd also instilled the fear that she would never be quite good enough to survive into adulthood.

Well, she had. On her own steam, too. Joining the Air Force and learning to fly had been the toughest thing she'd ever accomplished. At heart she wasn't military material—was too independent, too stubborn and free-spirited. But she'd sucked it up and completed her tour to achieve her goals. She'd done what she had to do and was damn proud of herself for getting through it.

Exasperation boiled into her throat and thinned her voice. "Of all the... I'm a big girl Jack. In case you hadn't noticed. I fly jumbo jets." What would it take for him to respect her capabilities?

"You change boyfriends like underwear."

Could she kill him and make it look like an accident? "You're the one who encourages me to do that. No one I choose can meet your standards."

"So it's wrong to have high standards?"

"You're not the only person who has them! I can judge for myself, you know."

"And look who you pick. I can't leave you alone for a second."

Kira took a few calming breaths. This conversation was utterly irrational, yet so typical of Jack. As her dad's star pupil, he'd always been overly protective of her. Had, in fact, enlisted her brother Mike to keep boys away from her in high school. It'd been ridiculous, the way they'd howled at the pimply boys who rang the doorbell. Whenever they got started, her only defense was to laugh, or turn the tables. "Would you rather me date bimbos, like you do?"

"It would be an improvement. Every time Arlo sees me at the airport he says *HiJack*."

A chill ran down her spine. Everyone was entitled to a momentary lapse in good taste, but few in the industry went *that* far.

"The bastard has no class."

She shrugged and swallowed her distaste. The jury was still out on Arlo, but she wasn't about to inform Jack of that fact. "At least he can remember your name."

"Wish I could forget his." Jack muttered quietly and crossed long, leanly muscled legs. "What kind of a name is *Arlo*, anyway?"

"Don't start."

"Doesn't sound good in a clench. Arlo," he trilled. "Oh, Arloooooooooo."

"Stop it." Kira giggled. She'd been practicing moaning Arlo's name in bed. The snickers still bubbled up, but things had improved to where she thought she could manage when and if the time came. God, she hated it when Jack hit the mark.

"There hasn't been a clench, right?"

Kira poked his thigh. "Mind your own beeswax. I'm twenty-eight years old."

Jack groaned, leaning forward to rip off another wedge of pizza and prep his mouth for stuffing. "Now you got me all worked up."

Kira stared at him. "You do this to yourself. Every time. Just forget about who I date and what I do on those dates. It's none of your business."

He swallowed the pizza. "It haunts me. At night. I can't sleep." He folded his arms and pouted.

Kira shook her head, watching him out of the corner of her eye. He looked cute that way, square bottom lip pressed tight over a dimpled chin. So unlike the Jack he presented to the world. As far as she knew, she was the only one who ever saw him like this—big hunk-o-man in a sulk.

It reminded her of how he'd looked when his mother threw him out as a teen. How he'd slumped into Kira's household and under her parents' watch—a shattered spirit lacquered in a fine sheen of bravado.

That was her Jack. Juvenile delinquent-turned Naval aviator-turned commercial pilot. Faithful friend.

They'd always been close. They'd shared a lust for adrenaline-pumping speed and the thrill of flight, which had, at Jack's urging, manifested itself into this new partnership at Pan Air. Tomorrow night, she'd make her maiden voyage. With Jack at the helm.

"There goes Julia running away again." Jack broke into Kira's thoughts and she focused glazed eyes on the TV. "The director must've been a fly on your bedroom wall."

"And if he was, he'd have seen you buzzing in to swat anything interesting that might've happened there."

Especially since her father had died. Right when she'd decided to fill the hole he'd left with a husband and maybe get started on a family of her own, Jack was always around, always pestering her, always popping in with a pizza—particularly when Arlo was here.

"He modeled Julia after you," Jack said.

"It's a movie, Jack. A movie." Kira clicked off the *Runaway Bride* before the DVD was half through. "I'm not watching this with you and your commentary."

"I don't make commentary."

"You just said she was like me."

Jack picked up the remote control and flicked it back on. "She is. Only not as pretty."

That shouldn't have pleased her but it did. Jack liked blondes. Kira was a blonde. It was a no-brainer he'd think her prettier than Julia Roberts, but she pumped a mental fist anyway.

"Turn it off. We're out of time." She still held a glimmer of hope Arlo would materialize this evening. Jack had to make himself scarce.

"I want to see how it ends."

"She gets married."

"Ruin my Friday night." Jack sprang off the couch, sauntered to the TV and popped the DVD out of the player. Turning in the blue light from the vacant screen, his plaid flannel shirttails wafted in the cool ocean breeze from the open window in her condo. Her gaze followed the movement and she looked out over Atlantic Beach. Surf pounded ominously, the wind picking up. A tropical storm was moving in and she and Jack with a flight tomorrow night. Not good.

Jack strode to the patio doors, leaned on the frame and let his gaze stray out into the sunset. "Might swing into Atlantic Beach," he mused. "I hate you living here."

Kira knew where this was going.

"You're on the first floor. When you went to buy this place, I told you—"

"Not the first floor," Kira said in tandem with Jack.

"And look. A hurricane," he said after a brief silence.

"You don't know that yet," she said.

"It's happened before."

If living with her father had taught her one thing, it was that pilots always had a contingency plan. There wasn't one emergency life had to offer that a pilot wouldn't think up plan B for. And Jack was a perfect example.

Kira hadn't realized until her father died that she didn't quite fit the mold. She was a fatalist, of sorts. Her attitude drove Jack up a wall. But what could she do? She wasn't going to live in fear of what might happen. When your time was up, it was up. "Jack. People's houses get destroyed. It's nature."

"Not when you live where nature wants you to live."

"And a high-rise in Manhattan is one of those places?" Okay, that was evil, but she made her point. Jack was devoted to his fortieth-floor view.

"That was an anomaly. People don't normally crash airplanes into skyscrapers, but hurricanes often blow condos apart."

"Okay. You're right. Someday the floods will come and wash away my condo. So what?"

"You'll be homeless."

Kira smiled sweetly. "I have you."

Jack rolled his eyes and pinched the bridge of his nose. "That's what I'm afraid of."

She got busy picking up the pizza box, paper plates and dirty napkins and carrying them to the kitchen trash. Jack followed with the empty beer bottles, tossing them into the recycling bin and grabbing two fresh, cold bottles from the fridge. He cracked one for her and handed it over, leaning back to lounge against the counter. "Where's Dicky Dweeb tonight?"

Kira took a sip and sat down at the table. A furtive glance at the clock told her Arlo should've called by now. He probably had a sensible excuse but her hopes sank. A continually silent phone never boded well for a relationship. She wasn't about to enlighten Jack, though. "I told you. He had a flight."

"Oh." Jack smirked. "Guess he's too tired."

"Will you can it?" Bad enough that Arlo'd stood her up without Jack gloating in her face. She sighed and rested chin in hand, wondering if she'd ever "get laid but good" as her friend Lea suggested. Not with Jack around. That's for sure. She looked at him. "You can go now."

His grin deepened, showcasing killer dimples and a flash of pearly whites. He really did have star quality, not that it did Kira any good, or that she cared. But she could appreciate his physical beauty objectively, in a platonic way. Nothing wrong with that.

Tall and leanly athletic, his graceful bod boasted broad shoulders and well-defined pecs. A classically handsome face contained watchful blue-raspberry colored eyes. Sometimes, she had to admit, she got a funny feeling in the pit of her stomach when he smiled. Like now. But she always shrugged it off. As her brother Mike once said, Jack could make any woman's stomach do the cha-cha.

Technically, he was Mike's best friend, and had been since high school. When Mike had slung a backpack over his shoulders and departed on the first of many personal sojourns to the mystical places of the world, common interests and mutual loneliness for his calm, insightful companionship had drawn Jack and Kira closer together. Though they both maintained a strong relationship with her brother—visiting him often at his sculpting studio in Colorado—it was Kira who bore the burden of Jack's considerable angst. And she wasn't as well-equipped to deal with it.

He had the energy equivalent of a stick of dynamite. His mother, unable to handle what would probably be diagnosed as OCD today, had simply given up and walked away. Good thing Kira's father had seen it coming. He'd invited Jack to live with them for the last two years of school, encouraged Jack to join the Navy and go to college. And look at him now.

Kira felt a burst of pride.

"I'll wait," Jack said, scraping out a chair and sitting on it backwards. He rested elbows on the table and stared at her—an unsettling habit he'd fallen into lately.

"Don't you have a home?"

"A real man wouldn't be too tired to see his woman."

"Maybe he was delayed."

"Let's find out." Jack flipped his cell phone open. "What's the flight number?"

Great. Calling her bluff. "I don't know."

He closed the phone and slipped it back into his breast pocket, piercing gaze still resting on her face. "What do you want with a quality assurance officer, anyway?"

"What do you want with a flight attendant?" Why were they having this conversation? Sure, Jack always poked his nose into her bedroom. Par for the course. But Arlo had somehow kicked his usual interest up a notch. If she didn't know better, she'd have thought he was jealous.

"Why don't you date pilots, like normal people?" he said.

Because between Jack and her father, she'd had it with the control freaks. "The last thing I need is another *you* in my life."

Jack rubbed his nose and sniffed. "I'm not so bad."

"Says who?"

Jack scratched at his beer label, loosening a corner and easing the paper skin off the moist surface in one deft sweep. "Bet Arlo can't do that." He grinned.

Kira laughed. "You're a man of many talents. Now go." If she didn't kick him out, he'd stay all night, monitoring her life, screening her calls, rooting through her medicine cabinet and critiquing her choice of pharmaceuticals.

"You have no idea," he said softly, and his bright gaze lifted from the crumpled label and thumbtacked her to her seat.

She swallowed hard as a little poof of breath dried her throat. Stay calm. Nothing to get alarmed about. Just Jack's eyes. "Arlo'll be here any minute. You have to go."

"I want to ask him something."

"I'll ask for you."

Jack's eyes narrowed and Kira felt a flash of triumph. Long fingers drummed the metal tabletop and Kira saw restlessness bunching in his muscles. Something was up. She could smell it. "What's with you tonight?"

He scraped back the chair so suddenly she jumped. "I wonder what he wants with you." He hopped up and started pacing, massaging the back of his neck.

"Thanks a lot."

"That's not what I meant." Jack stopped and pointed at her. "He's not a safe bet."

"I'll be the judge of that."

"If Pan Air's budget goes south, so will his job."

"Okay, Mr. Bulletproof."

"Kira." He came around the table and spun her chair so she faced him. "This isn't a joke."

The fervid concern on his face did her in and she slumped, antagonism seeping away on the fresh ocean breeze. Jack might be a PITA, but he did have her best interests at heart. More importantly, he'd never leave her in peace if she didn't smooth his feathers somehow. "Arlo's not coming," she admitted. "He would've called first."

Jack continued inspecting her face for a moment before cursing low in his throat and turning away. "I'll rip him a new one."

"I thought you'd be glad."

"No. You stand the asshole up, not the other way around. I'll kill him."

"One minute you're accusing me of being the Queen of Disposable Men, the next minute you want me to dump another one. You're insane."

"You made me that way."

Kira stood up and stretched, moving behind Jack where he stood at the window. Her eyes fell even with his shoulders and she could see the smooth flannel hugging every muscle. She inhaled and euphoria exploded in her brain. He smelled like pressurized air, nighttime and the sky. Most pilots smelled the same way, only with aftershave undertones. Jack just smelled of the elements. "Go get some sleep. See you at the airport?"

He reached back and hooked an arm over her shoulders, tugging her next to him in a warm embrace. "I'll pick you up."

"Sounds good."

"Scared?"

"About flying with you? God yes."

He guffawed and dropped a firm kiss on her forehead. "I'll go easy on you."

"Right."

"I will." His voice had grown deeper and held a hint of a tease. She looked up, meaning to razz him back, and caught him on the downswing as his lips pressed hers in their signature goodnight smooch. Teeth collided. Eyes flew open and lips curled against each other in a smile.

Kira meant to blink and pull away, but his pupils—big as the night sky—wrapped around her. Suddenly, she wasn't gazing into Jack's blue-raspberry eyes anymore. Instead, she was falling into swirling, blue-black holes. Tiny sparklers backlit them—like twinkling stars outside an inky cockpit. The galaxy of emotion she glimpsed galvanized her, shooting an afterburn down her thighs.

His lips softened ever so slightly, and the afterburn spread like wildfire into her arms, her chest and heart. Against her wishes, her lips parted in response.

With a faint, vibrating groan, he tightened his grip on her shoulder, stiffly pulling her closer as if fighting an unseen and opposing force.

"Jack?" she murmured.

He released her.

Succulent lips unlatched and they pulled away as slowly and reluctantly as two magnets.

An odd look flinched across his features. Kira stepped back and automatically sent a hand to straighten her long, blonde hair.

"Be ready at seven," he said thickly. He turned toward the front door, yanked it open and hesitated for a microsecond on the threshold. Kira swore his hand trembled on the doorknob. His head swiveled slightly. She glimpsed a tight profile. His lips parted. Then he left.

She felt like she'd been stuffed with wet wool.

In a locked closet in her mind, she screamed this couldn't be happening again. Flashback twelve years ago, to Jack's goodbye kiss as he left for Naval training, and how it had somehow spun out of control there in the garage, him pinning her against the car door, the welcome relief of his hands finally on her…

He'd written her a jokey, flirtatious letter afterwards leaving no doubt in her mind that the kiss held no importance to him whatsoever. She'd joked about it right back, to cover her wounded pride. So they'd gone along, being the same as always—except in those occasional glances he sent her, and how he wedged himself between her and all her boyfriends.

If she was the Queen of Disposable Men, Jack was the court executioner.

So what now?

Call Lea. She would know what to do. Kira crossed to the lemon-yellow wall phone and dialed her friend's number.

"Emergency pig-out," she announced into the answering machine, hanging up in frustration and feeling hollow. Lea must be out on a date. It was the one constant in the universe.

Somehow, the thought of running out for her own chocolate binge—alone—didn't have the same allure. Too bad her mother, Maggie, lived on the opposite end of Long Island. One hundred miles never seemed so far away. Then again, this wasn't exactly something she could talk to her mother about.

Yeah, Mom, I just realized I want to boink Jack. Can I? Huh? Can I?

Flinging herself to the fridge in frustration, Kira rooted through the freezer section and unearthed a one-pound brick of Cadbury. Great. Jack had gotten if for her on his last flight to London. She couldn't eat it without thinking of him, and right now, he was the last person she wanted to think about.

Arlo. Dream of Arlo. Right. Hard to fantasize about a man who only thought of Trojans as computer viruses. At least Jack had testosterone.

Crap.

The phone rang.

"Got your message but I'm...tied up right now," Lea's voice came through the line.

"Literally, I'm sure."

Lea snickered and a muffled noise in the background made Kira wonder.

"Give me a quick rundown."

"I had a *moment* with Jack." Kira twirled the phone cord between damp fingers.

The line sizzled. "A sexual moment?"

Kira nodded before realizing Lea couldn't see her. It didn't matter, Lea could sense sex a world away.

"This is so wrong on so many levels," Lea said. "I mean, he's like your brother—"

"He's *not* my brother," Kira wailed. "That's just it. Even though sometimes it feels like he is."

"If it smells like a brother and feels like a brother, it is a brother. I can't listen to this."

"Will you stop joking and cut me a break? I feel awful. I mean it was there. A spark. Something. This can't be happening."

"Put it out of your mind."

Kira rested a hot forehead against the cool plastic phone. A quick glance around the airy condo assured her of familiar surroundings, lending a comfort to the tumultuous emotions roiling in her brain. There was the orange, nubby thrift shop sofa. Beside it sat a turquoise fiberglass chair—complete with purple seat cushion.

"Don't panic. Okay?"

Kira heard deep, raspy laughter, a giggle and the sounds of flesh slapping flesh. "Lea, what are you doing?"

Did she really want to know?

Bright yellow walls enveloped her with warmth, and on sunny afternoons, with the misty light streaming in, she could almost glimpse Nirvana. Right here on a New York beach.

Jack had helped her decorate, complaining vigorously at each junk store stop, every curbside find. But he'd dutifully loaded her treasures in his BMW, carried them inside, and now, seemed to prefer her condo to his own glossy, Upper East Side bachelor pad.

Funny how it worked out that way.

Lea's strident, feminine voice pulled her back to reality. "Look. I can't talk right now—"

The connection crackled, gasped and died. Kira started to slam the receiver down, but stopped herself in time. Wonderful. Just wonderful. Cast adrift in the Sea of Jack with no rudder, not even an anchor.

A gust of wind blew hair into her face and she went to close the window. Staring through her reflection, she caught the first trailings of Mare's Tails in the sky. Cirrus clouds. The precursors of a storm.

At least Jack would have something besides Arlo to gripe about tomorrow night, she thought. Tropical storms were nothing to sneeze at when it came to flying.

Kira moved around the condo, switched off the lights, washed her face and snuggled beneath a summer-weight comforter with the window next to her bed cracked. Exhaustion glued her limbs to the sheets and her eyelids fluttered shut. Only then did she remember it was not only a seven-hour flight, alone with Jack, but a thirty-six-hour layover as well.

Alone. With Jack.

Chapter Two

Moral dilemma number two –
Can you fool around with your best friend and then pretend it never happened?

Jack hauled Kira's luggage off the crew bus and wheeled it to the curb, turning to make sure she'd follow him inside the airport. As if she wouldn't, moron. He had to get a grip.

Ever since that kiss last night he couldn't tell his ass from his elbow. It'd taken every last ounce of reserve he possessed not to bring it up in the car, rehash the details, figure out what the hell had happened between them.

And of course, she'd been no help, peering at him from under her cap with those cat-like green eyes, looking away when he opened his yap to say something and generally behaving as if nothing had happened at all.

Maybe it didn't. Maybe it'd been his own twisted imagination, a nightmare brought on by the image of her marrying that squirrelly bastard Arlo.

Jack clenched her suitcase handle and he felt the hard plastic snap a little. God. He told her to get the nylon grip, but no –

Ease up, Grayson.

He had her in his sights now. Oh yeah. He'd kept his promise to the old man and that was something to hang onto.

Kira wouldn't take any more flights without him, wouldn't be stuck with a sphincter in the hot seat if things went south, and most importantly, she wouldn't marry a middle-management schmuck.

It was a tall order, but Jack was willing to shoulder it—for now.

After all, the old man saved his ass, which would've certainly turned to grass if he'd gone after his mother. Jack owed everything he had to Tom Allen. Everything. And he would honor his deathbed vow to take care of Kira until he could unload her on someone worthwhile.

Maybe that sounded old-fashioned, but it was Tom's idea, not Jack's. Jack was just being indulgent. Never mind that Tom couldn't be indulged anymore, since he was dead. Jack felt it was the right thing to do.

"Let's go."

They strolled through the airport, black luggage rolling neatly to heel. Kira set off babe alarms in that uniform and Jack felt his chest swell with pride.

Her silky, blonde ponytail swung low underneath her cap, secured with a metal clip bearing the Pan Air winged globe. When she tilted her face to tell him something, her vivid green eyes held a sparkle of intelligence he'd scouted in other women, but failed to find, and she was the only woman he'd ever known who could keep up with him both mentally and physically. He savored every second he spent with her. She was so damn unique, his little bud.

"Hold a sec. I need a book." Kira veered across the concourse toward a magazine stand while Jack appreciated the rear view. Earlier, when he'd helped her into the Beemer, he'd noticed she had one fine tail rotor.

He tilted his head. Round and smooth—and deadly if you got too close.

Jack pulled up beside her so he couldn't see her ass. It was the only way he could think of to cool off.

That, and talking. "Aren't we going to talk?"

Kira put down one book and picked up another. "Sure."

"Then why the book?"

"I need something at the hotel."

Jack looked at the cover. It had half-naked people on it, male and female. In bed. "You can't buy that."

Kira followed his eyes and smirked. "Jealous?" She licked her lips and Jack's jet poked its nose out of the hangar. "I thought I might pick up some pointers," she added.

Shit.

Under any other circumstances, his comeback would've been, *Pick me up and I'll give you those pointers.* And he would've moved in. Quick.

But this was Kira.

"They'd be wasted on Arlo," he said instead, trying to shutter his mind to the image of Kira and Arlo.

"Then who would you suggest?" Kira asked, eyes bright and challenging.

Too late. The image seeped in and his chest tightened. He hated the pencil-pushing prick. Kira needed a real man in bed. She needed, "Him".

"Who?"

No, no, no.

Not him.

Someone *like* him. But he hated men like him, too. In fact, he hated all men—especially the multitudes sniffing around Kira.

"The guy on the book," he muttered lamely.

She threw him a narrow glance and he raised his eyebrows at her in an attempt to appear innocent. She seemed to buy it.

"Be right back," she clipped.

Saved. For the moment. Now if only he could forget that luscious ass and how it might feel between his teeth.

Jack white-knuckled the bookshelf while Kira paid the cashier. He wanted to get rid of her, not have sex with her. If he had sex with her, he'd be enslaved for the rest of his natural life.

That's bad? Jack shook his head—hard. Kira might be every man's erotic fantasy. But she wasn't his. Nope. No way.

"Ready?"

He nodded. They continued down the concourse to the gate. If Mike knew what he'd been thinking, he'd skin him alive. Tom would rise from the grave to feed his balls to the polar bears at the Bronx Zoo, while Jack watched.

He'd been warned. And the Allens were not to be messed with. Of course the warning had come twelve years prior, when Jack had snagged her for a goodbye kiss and lived to regret it. Barely.

He'd never forgotten the aftermath, sitting across from them at the table as they outlined how he would die, and how long it would take.

Good thing he'd convinced Kira to expand her career horizons. With any luck, she'd fall in love in a major west coast metropolis—or Tasmania—move there and disappear. Then Jack's job would be done. He could have peace. Total freedom. And that's exactly what he wanted.

*****

Inside the aircraft cabin, the cleaning crew, catering service and flight attendants were bustling. After greeting them, Kira stowed her cockpit case and handed Jack the weather printouts so he could map the route.

So far, so good, she told herself, proud that she'd maintained a professional distance for the ride to the airport. The whole time, she'd seen the wheels turning in Jack's head. He couldn't seem to figure out what to say to her, and she had no clue either, so she'd decided to take Lea's advice and put it out of her head.

A red-eye in a storm was not a good arena in which to get emotional. Plenty of time later to talk about *The Kiss*, if it needed talking about by then. It wasn't as if she wanted to get involved with Jack, anyway. She couldn't even imagine how controlling he'd be as a lover.

Lover. An unwanted image of them both in a tangle, his hands fisting in her hair, the warm slide of flesh on flesh…

"Winds gusting to thirty knots. Piece of cake. We'll go up to Wisconsin and across for the pit stop in Spokane," he said. "With any luck, the weather will hold and we won't get diverted to Idaho."

Snapped back to reality, Kira pulled a face. Spokane's fog was almost as unpredictable as London's. "Remember sitting on the runway at Shannon?" On one of their many adventures they'd taken a mini-vacation to England five years ago, encountered thick fog and ended up spending most of the one full day they had on the tarmac in Ireland.

"Oh yeah." Jack smirked. "How about the time we came home through D.C. and barely caught the last train to New York."

She'd almost forgotten. "Those were the days." She and Jack gallivanting around the world on employee passes, hooking up with Mike and his Druid friends at Stonehenge, snorting beer with mountain climbers in Interlaken. She and Jack…

Kira jumped when his fingers gripped her elbow and her eyes flew up from the charts to meet his. The confines of the flight deck, coupled with their cap brims colliding, cast shadows across his face and darkened his eyes.

"We had some good times," he said.

"Sure did." When had his voice gotten so raspy?

Jack cleared his throat. "Better file the flight plan and prepare the cockpit."

His hands dropped and slipped around her waist and they performed a makeshift tango so he could fold his lean body into the coveted left seat.

As they twisted, Kira felt something long and hard brush her hip. Though she broke out in a sweat, she didn't spare herself congratulations. Pilots could be armed, now. So it might truly have been a pistol in his pocket.

Still, she felt shaky and claustrophobic, so she waved over her shoulder from the cockpit door.

"I'm going out for the visual inspection."

"Bring your glue gun," Jack said.

Out on the tarmac, she shoved thoughts of Jack aside and strolled around the plane, checking valves, fan blades and engine struts. She eyeballed the tail area and the entire fuselage, stopping at the landing gear to inspect the tires and hydraulic lines.

Lord she loved being underneath a jumbo jet, using her eyes, her knowledge and her gut to ensure flight worthiness. The aroma of jet fuel always kick-started her adrenaline, adventure distilled to its purest form—taking people into the stratosphere where they had no business being. Then bringing them back. Alive.

No matter how many trips she took, the speed of jet travel still awed her. She glanced at the moon, blown away that within hours she'd be in Seattle. While passengers slept, she and Jack would be watching out for them, delivering them safely, taking their trust, and, hopefully, their luggage.

She passed around the nose of the giant jet, waving up at Jack as she ducked underneath. As usual, everything checked out and she drew a satisfied breath and returned to the cockpit.

"Bucket-o-bolts?" Jack asked.

He handed her a clipboard and she settled into her seat to begin the preflight checklist. Withdrawing a pen from her breast pocket, she glanced at him and automatically wet the tip of the pen with her tongue—a habit left over from childhood.

Jacks eyelids fell to half-mast. He leaned a shoulder against the window, turning toward her as much as he could in the cramped space. "Don't do that," he murmured and his voice rippled through her like a moan.

"Do what?"

"Lick the pen."

Kira blinked as her face heated and a warm flush spread over her chest. What was going on here? This was

Jack, for crying out loud. But it wasn't. At least not the Jack she knew.

This Jack looked hungry and hot, ever since they boarded. Couldn't be because of Kira. Must be Svetlana, the dishy blonde flight attendant.

"Aye, aye," she said and snapped him a salute. Think business, not about Jack Grayson and how ravenous he looked right now. "L/G lever."

"Down."

"Flaps."

"Up."

Svetlana dripped in with coffee, forgetting Kira's cream but getting Jack's exactly right.

"Engine Bleed Valve."

"On."

Svetlana returned with the cream and Kira balanced the checklist on her thigh. Jack steadied it with one finger while she doctored the watery brew. Even through the stainless steel, Kira felt the pressure of his fingertip. So concentrated, so focused. And it shimmered up her thigh like a ribbon of heated breath. "Fuel Transfer Main."

"Off."

She shot him a glance. "You didn't check that one."

"Check it yourself."

What was with him? "Let's finish this so I can play hostess."

Jack acted like her demands were too outrageous, but he sighed and went back to business. Finally, it was meet-and-greet time. She got up and stood outside the open cockpit door.

As the passengers dispersed to their seats and wrestled with the overhead bins, Kira spotted a tall, familiar form strolling down the jetway. She blinked and refocused. Would wonders never cease?

Arlo. Coming to watch her and Jack?

"Evening," he said, drawing to a stop at the door and giving the hinges a once-over. To her surprise, Kira bristled. The visual inspection was her domain.

"Hey! Long time no see," she said steadily, smoothing her uniform jacket and resisting the urge to do the same to her ponytail.

He wore an official-looking black suit with tie, and, under a mop of sand-colored hair, an equally official expression in his deep, brown eyes. So much for tongue kissing in the lavatory.

"Been busy, but thought I'd tag along on your first flight," he said. "Word on the street is you're good." He winked at her and she felt her smile brightening. His easygoing nature shrouded her in a field of calm and she was suddenly deliriously grateful to have him on board to balance her wayward emotions and distract her from Jack's overwhelming allure.

Speaking of whom. Out of the corner of her eye, she saw him glance over his shoulder and do a comical double take. *Fasten your seatbelts*.

Jack unfolded from the left seat and joined them at the door.

"Grayson," Arlo said.

Was it her imagination, or did Jack's lip curl back?

"Jacobs." Jack nodded. Only Kira seemed to notice it came out sounding like *jackass*.

The two men faced each other down and Kira felt her head go woozy. They were both attractive in utterly opposing ways, and watching them posturing, taking each other's measure, she was nearly overcome by testosterone fumes.

It gave her hope to see that Arlo had some. Maybe for the last few dates he'd been holding back, being a gentleman. Maybe soon he'd unleash it in a more private arena…

She and Jack exchanged glances and she saw thunder in his eyes. She glared back at him and his eyes narrowed, silent subtext zinging back and forth between them. Slowly, Jack eased into the phoniest smile she'd ever seen.

"Buckle up, *Arlo*. Ms. Allen's about to give you the ride of your life."

"I'd like to take a look at your performance first, Jack," Arlo primly replied. "Pan Air discourages first-timers from taking the controls in questionable weather."

A pregnant pause.

Kira's shoulder muscles bunched.

"Are you saying you can judge Kira's abilities better than the FAA?" Jack growled. He took a menacing step forward and Arlo stood his ground.

She reached out and gripped Jack's arm. "It's okay, Jack. Let him do his job."

Arlo reached into his breast pocket and pulled out his glasses. "Thank you, Kira. I knew I could count on you to see the complexities here. Now. I would prefer it if Jack handled the take-off for this leg of the flight."

"We'll let her control the crash then."

Kira cringed as Arlo winced. Jack considered landings to be nothing more than controlled crashes, but usually he was smart enough to keep that information to himself, and out of hearing of passengers and Quality Assurance Officers.

Arlo jotted a quick note on his clipboard. Jack dug himself a deeper hole. "Hours of boredom sandwiched between two minutes of sheer terror."

"Jack," she said through her teeth. She'd never seen him act so unprofessionally in front of corporate suits. What was his problem?

Again, the specter that he might actually be jealous, that his prejudice against Arlo went deeper than Arlo's position at Pan Air, rushed at her. And splattered against a brick wall in her psyche. It simply couldn't be.

Jack tossed her a surly glance and slanted himself back into his seat. Kira followed suit and as their heads bumped while they shifted to get comfortable, Jack snarled in her ear, "I'm not canceling our tour tomorrow so you can cozy up to that shit-for-brains."

They'd booked a whale watching expedition that Kira had looked forward to, but now she felt obligated to spend time with Arlo. No, not obligated. She *wanted* to spend time with him, get to know him better. He might be a tad undercooked on the surface, but he had the quiet, soothing qualities she thought she craved in a mate.

"We made those plans before I knew he would be on board," she whispered.

"So what?"

"Let's invite him along," she suggested. What else could she do? It seemed impolite to run off with Jack when Arlo had taken the trouble to be on her flight. Then again, he hadn't exactly warned her, or asked for a date in Seattle.

A few choice curses spewed out of Jack right when Arlo entered the flight deck to sit on the jump seat. He didn't appear to hear. Thank God.

Jack's cheekbones flushed an uncharacteristic shade of cranberry and Kira had to check twice to convince herself of what she was seeing. "Jack—"

"Ready?" he said, jaw twitching.

He was pissed. Well, so what?

They looked at each other for a long, silent moment, the angry lick of his eyes on her face. Finally, he held up his hand like an arm wrestler. Kira looped her arm around his and their fingers meshed tightly. "Ready."

"Working with you is quite the experience." He gave her hand a fierce, hard kiss then donned his headset and his easy-going pilot voice. "This is Pan Air two-oh-seven. Aircraft ready for pushback. Request pushback."

They taxied to the end of the runway and, with Arlo's careful gaze upon her, Kira ticked off the items on the taxi checklist. Jack obtained takeoff clearance, advanced the throttles and started the roll.

Watching Jack barrel a million pounds of people and explosive fuel down the pavement had Kira's blood pounding in rhythm with the wheels. Her gaze flitted across the instrument panel, noting pressure readings and flap angles, and these she recorded on autopilot. But it was the exhilaration of taking off with Jack that dominated her consciousness.

Everything had changed. The disquieting sexual snap between them hadn't lingered this long before and like the airplane gusting into the sky, she felt as if she was being launched somewhere she wasn't supposed to be.

Chapter Three

Moral dilemma number three –
Does getting to know your enemy qualify as an excuse to sleep with him?

"What now, Svetlana?" Kira said an hour later as an obscenely long leg appeared at her side for the umpteenth time. Her teeth ached when a manicured hand rested on Jack's shoulder.

"Do you need anything?" the blonde asked, rotating slender hips and sending a light floral scent through the flight deck.

"Not at the moment," Jack said, turning from his charts to glance up at her.

Kira watched his eyes carefully, for the fire she'd glimpsed earlier. But Jack's expression was as blank as they came. Interesting.

"I'd like a club soda," she put in. "Thanks for asking."

Svetlana's smile faltered. "Of course. Mr. Jacobs?"

Kira caught a flash of white as Arlo grinned up at Svetlana. "I'll help you get the beverages," he said.

What was that strange glitter in his eye?

As the door latched behind them, Kira whipped her head back around toward the instrument panel. Fast. Jealousy pierced her. Arlo never looked at her like that. No one looked at her like that. Except—

When she glanced at Jack he had his pen light out and had returned to his maps. The velvet darkness of outer space on the other side of the window acted as a foil for his crisp profile, sleekly wavy hair and broad, capable shoulders.

Her mouth watered. His physical perfection slammed her backwards. Always had. But she'd gotten used to it over the years and had managed to weigh it unfavorably against his peskiness.

Tonight it had taken on a personal meaning. Comparing him to Arlo earlier, she'd realized not only was Jack desirable to the female population in general, he was desirable to *her*. He messed with every one of her senses, fucked with her serenity. And now with the way he kept eyeing her, staring into her, probing... She couldn't think straight and appraise anyone else fairly with him on top of her all the time.

She swallowed and promised herself that during this trip, she would transfer these sick, unwanted yearnings she had for an entirely inappropriate man, and direct them where they belonged. She also intended to douse the heat in Jack's eyes, and reignite it in Arlo's. For her. And only her.

"Did we grow a new land mass? You've been studying that map for thirty minutes." Her voice sounded brittle. But, whatever.

"Storm system's massive," Jack said. "Closing in on the Carolina coast."

"Hurricane?"

"Close." He folded the map and slid it into his case. "Not time to worry yet."

"Well, it's the season," she said, not especially concerned. Worst-case scenario would be another night in Seattle.

The cockpit door squeaked. Kira smelled Svetlana before she saw her and took the club soda before she'd set one sculpted foot inside. Jack snatched it and downed half.

"Hey! Get your own."

"When?" he asked between gulps. "Must be busy back there, haven't seen anyone all night."

"She offered you drinks five times."

He frowned. "No way."

Kira held up five fingers and Jack blinked, snapping his head toward the door, as if checking to make sure it worked. "She couldn't have."

"You just now told her you didn't want anything." He'd been looking through the hottest babe at Pan Air, giving Kira a glimpse into a whole new dimension of Jack.

Kira'd run into Svetlana at a handful of Jack's rooftop barbeques. She'd had a different escort each time and had never made an obvious play for Jack before tonight. Perhaps she'd practiced on everyone else before gunning for the big prize. "I can't believe you didn't notice."

"What's to notice?" He shrugged and held up the cup. "Want some?"

"No. What's not to notice?" Was he playing hard to get? Could this be his MO? She'd never paid attention to Jack's romantic methods. Suddenly, she wanted to know how he operated, if he was in fact interested and if ignoring the flight attendant was an intentional ploy to drive her wild. Kira'd never understood how inattentive men drew women in hoards. It had the opposite affect on her. Still, did it work well for Jack? Is that how she should behave with Arlo?

"About what?"

She sighed. "Svetlana, you dope."

"Are you asking if I have the hots for Svetlana?" Jack shook the plastic cup and bit into a chunk of ice.

"Don't you?" Seemed all her men did. Arlo hadn't come back.

With his mouth full of ice, Jack shook his head. "Too much mileage," he mumbled.

That made her giggle. "She'd be broken in by now."

Jack grinned, the dimples around his mouth sculpting and framing that sexy piece of art. "But she's lost that new car smell."

They howled. Talk about an unexpected development. Because he'd been so loud about her love life and silent about his own, she'd never had the energy to wonder what sort of woman, besides blonde, he preferred. Obviously, he didn't want a fast one, though she strongly suspected he'd been there done that. What *did* he want? Why did she care? At the moment, she had more important issues to attend. She stopped laughing. "I wonder if Arlo plans on taking Svet for a test drive."

Jack's grin faded too. "If he does, I'll pound him into the ground."

"You're a walking oxymoron, you know that? I'll never understand the way you think."

"Simple," Jack said, and crunched another chunk of ice. "If he cheats on you or mistreats you in any way, shape or form, he's prop wash."

Kira shuddered, thinking of the debris fields on runways—things that got caught and mangled in propellers. "What I don't understand is why you wouldn't be glad if he cheated on me. Because I'd break up with him."

Jack shot a finger at her. "Get something straight, Kira. I don't want you to marry that clown, but if you do anyway, I'll be watching and waiting. When the opportunity presents itself, if he makes a mistake—" He curled the finger into a fist and smacked it into his hand. Staring at the moon for a moment, his face caught the pale light and appeared ghostly. "You're really serious about him?" he asked quietly. "He's the one you want?"

Something in his tone captured her. Since her voice wouldn't work, she nodded.

In the dim light from the instruments, Jack's gaze wandered around her, stroking every feature. Desire spiraled through her system, wreaking havoc in her frontal lobe and causing her heart to lurch.

When he reached out and tucked a wisp of hair behind her ear, she experienced a powerful urge to turn into his palm, but his touch felt gentle and tentative and so unlike her forthright Jack that she hesitated.

His hand dropped. "Where would I fit into this sick little triangle?"

"What do you mean?" she croaked.

Jack turned his face away and his shoulders fell. "Are you going to dump me?"

"Of course not!"

He snorted.

"Jack," she whispered. "You're my best friend. Like a brother—"

His head snapped around and the bonfire in his eyes torched the cockpit. "I'm not your fucking brother!"

She drew back, scorched. In all the years she'd known him, he'd never acknowledged that fact in so many words.

Quite the opposite. Usually he insisted on being a family member with the vehemence of a junkyard dog protecting its territory.

Kira ran a visual over the instrument panel, absorbing this disturbing turnabout. Something strange was brewing in his head. She fought the urge to react with equal violence because a small corner of her brain registered pain, not anger, in his voice. Could he be afraid? Jack, afraid?

Hardly. More likely he was experiencing a snotty reaction to not getting his own way. Still, she wanted him to know she was sympathetic, so she pressed her palm against his cheek. "You okay?"

Suspended in the ink of night with stars splattered across the windscreen and the gentle, insistent hum of the engines vibrating underfoot, Jack froze at her touch.

"I'm not sure anymore," he murmured. "Are you?"

He had that glittering, predatory look again. This was getting bizarre. A sudden thickness in her throat made it difficult to breathe. "If you're okay, I'm okay."

He tilted his head into her hand, forcing her fingers through his hair. Kira couldn't prevent a little whimper as the silky strands flowed through her fingers.

Jack slid a hand along her arm to her shoulder, forming a bridge between them as he rubbed the nape of her neck. "What's happening here?"

God he felt good, his hands on her, his soft words wrapping around her like a lover. She didn't want this moment to end, wanted more. "You tell me."

He twisted out of his seat and yanked her up and before she knew it, his hands were everywhere and he was kissing her.

* * * * *

Jack wrapped his arms around her waist, pulling her soft, luscious breasts against him and pinning her between the seat and his raging erection.

What now? he thought as he slipped his tongue into that hot, wet mouth. *How am I going to get out of this one?*

Warning bells went wild in his brain. Kira was his buddy, his pal, not his sex toy. But the idea of her wanting someone else had proved too hot to handle. She was gorgeous, intelligent—everything *he* wanted right here, right now. And everything he didn't want. Ever.

Kira was pizza and beer, Friday night movies and globe-hopping. But she was also marriage and family, and someone to keep happy. Because Jack knew what happened when you pissed a woman off.

He also knew he was a royal pain in the ass. Kira told him so every day and he agreed. How long would it take her to get sick of him if they hooked up? None of Kira's men ever lasted very long, and he would be no different.

Her soft mews of pleasure shuddered through his body like slow, easy sex. She sounded that way when she ate something she liked, now he knew how she'd sound with him. Good God! Her hands roamed his back and he felt her fingernails gripping through his shirt.

Jack dropped his hand to her rump and locked her hips against his. She opened for him and his head exploded. Her warm lips wrapped around his, and those endless legs straddled his thighs, sending him into a tailspin of needy ecstasy. He reached down and grabbed them, hoisting her onto the armrest. Her legs went around his waist and she sucked his tongue into her mouth, twirling it with hers and driving him stark raving mad.

"Kira," he groaned, nipping at her hungrily. She tilted her head and he went for her throat, licking and tasting everything that was Kira.

Her breath came in small gasps as he thrust against her, hips meeting as eagerly as if they were naked, as if he could actually slip inside. And that was going to happen next—oh yeah. Right here.

Her reaction blew his mind. If he'd had to take a wild guess, he'd never have guessed she wanted him this badly. But she did, and she was proving it—every moan, every lick, every suckle on his skin making him crazier and crazier over the time they had wasted.

Jack unbuttoned her slacks, slipping a hand down her panties and shuddering when he realized how slick she was. Her hands wound urgently through his hair, cradling his head against her neck, and she burrowed to nibble his shoulder.

"Jack. Do it now."

He plunged his fingers inside and sucked on her neck, and she moaned, unbuttoning his pants, sliding in a hand, going down…

"Pan Air two-oh-seven, do you read?" A faraway voice floated into his consciousness as her fingers hovered over his erection.

Shit.

"Pan Air two-oh-seven, do you read?"

Jack tore out of Kira's arms, snapped on his headset and slid into his seat, dodging her as she did the same.

"Two-oh-seven, I do copy. What's happening?"

"Ascend to thirty-nine-thousand. That's ascend to thirty-nine-thousand."

"Roger."

Jack made the adjustments and stared into the night, unable to look at her. His heart was beating the band and his cock was about to detonate. How had he gone all this time without pawing Kira? And why did it have to happen now, on a thirty-six-hour layover?

There'd be no way to avoid her. They'd planned outings all over Seattle. He could get sick, but no one would buy that. He never got sick.

He'd have to foist her off on Arlo after all. All that careful planning down the crapper.

Great job keeping your promise to Tom, moron.

His chest tightened.

What the hell had he been thinking? He hadn't, that was the problem. He'd been reacting. To her and her sexy ass, and to some crushing, nameless dread. He was in for it now. Had no one to blame but himself and his treacherous F-16. Little bastard.

"Well, I guess you told me," Kira finally said in her I'm-gonna-be-brave voice.

Jack closed his eyes. That voice always killed him. She so rarely used it, and when she did, she really needed him. Unfortunately, he couldn't be there for her this time. Fucking asshole that he was. "At least now I know what's happening," he said softly.

They were silent for a minute.

"So what are we going to do about it?"

He turned to her, kicking himself for what he was about to say but unable to think of anything else. Better nip it now before it got too late. *It's already too late*. "How about nothing?"

Her gorgeous eyes widened then narrowed. She licked him off her lips and nodded curtly. "Sounds like a plan." Stiffly, she faced forward and ran an eye over the instrument panel. "Great night for flying."

He muttered a curse. "Kira—"

She showed him the hand. "I'm a big girl."

"It's not that I don't want to—"

"Then what is it?" she spat, turning on him like a frightened, hissing kitten.

He couldn't very well tell her he wanted to screw her brains out then send her packing. So what could he say? "I don't know."

The weight of her stare nearly crushed him. She stayed silent so long he began to twitch. "Forget it then," she bit out. "It was only a kiss."

"That was no ordinary kiss." He had to go and bring it up.

"To whom?"

Slap. Okay, he deserved it. Panic clogged his pipeworks. He hated fearing what an angry woman might do, avoided it like the plague. This was exactly the reason he never wanted to get hitched. "I don't want us to change."

"We won't."

Why did he not believe her? Maybe because the air surrounding her felt so clotted with hostility it refused to circulate. *Stop looking at me that way.*

"It was bound to happen sometime." She shrugged. "Chalk it up to a moment of insanity in outer space."

"You sure?"

"Jack. It's no big deal. Okay?"

Ouch. Right. No big deal. "Roger that."

"I'm going to the bathroom."

He stayed glued to his chair, paralyzed from the waist down. Underneath the spitting venom, her voice had sounded burnt. Crispy. Hurt. He'd committed a cardinal sin. He'd scorned her. What was she going to do next? Payback was certainly a bitch and Jack harbored no hope of escaping Hell's fury.

His neck bones cracked like a walnut as he rolled it from side to side. In the Navy he'd shot the most sophisticated artillery known to humankind and skimmed bleeding aircraft over killer waves. All without losing his cool. Wasn't it a fucking bitch that one angry woman could reduce him to a puddle of chicken shit.

*****

Man-oh-man did she want to immolate him now. Kira slammed the lavatory door and rammed the lock. Of all the lame stunts.

"How about nothing." She made a face and mimicked his words. *"I don't want us to change."* Too late, Bucko. The imprint of his erection had fossilized between her legs. Hard, hot and ready for action. With her. And man did she want it. Fast and sweaty. With Jack.

She looked in the mirror, cursed, and unclipped her hair. Had anyone seen her as she dodged into the lav? God. She hoped not. She looked like a train wreck. No mistaking what she'd been up to with Jack. Flushed cheeks, check. Feverish eyes, check. And a crotch that glowed like a rotisserie grill. Thank heavens no one could see *that*.

Good God she wanted Jack to see it, to touch it again, to rotate his fingers and his cock until done. Eat. Then do it all over again.

Steady girl.

There was no doubt left in her mind that Jack was jealous of Arlo. Even if he didn't know it himself. Even if he'd never admit it. The jealousy was eating him up and driving him to commit uncharacteristic deeds.

But what kind of jealousy was it? Territorial? Misplaced protectiveness? A lover's?

How would she ever find out?

And she needed to, in order to proceed with her life. She needed to know how to handle Jack's explosive reactions.

As well as her own.

Otherwise how could she ever marry someone else? He'd be always skulking, waiting to get her in a closet, trying to lure her away from her marriage vows—whether he meant to or not.

She gazed at her reflection in the mirror. Saucer-sized eyes stared back at her in the pasty fluorescent light.

And it looked like he could do it, too.

She licked her lips, savoring the last remnants of his flavor. Her fingers smelled of his shampoo, and a heavier elemental essence all his own. It surrounded her in the tiny lav, wafting up from her neck where he'd lapped her skin, blowing out of her hair as she combed it into the ponytail.

Jack was everywhere.

Bracing shaky hands on the sink, Kira bowed her head and took several fortifying breaths. She didn't want to sleep with him. She needed to remember that. It'd been a long time since she had sex and, writhing in the throes of a tantric tantrum, her buddy Jack was looking mighty fine right now. That's all it was. Nothing more.

Once she was safely married to a rational man and having regular blowout sex, she'd be fine.

You could have regular, blowout sex with Jack.

No.

All he needs is a tiny shove…

Jack irritated her beyond belief. Barely tolerable in his present state, he'd be insufferable as a lover. Wouldn't he? She searched the mirror for answers she was too horny to find. Wouldn't he?

The seatbelt light dinged. A powerful jolt knocked her into the wall and she reckoned she'd better get back to work.

As she unlocked the door and swayed into the aisle, Arlo caught her by the elbow.

"I was worried," he said, opening the cockpit door for her. "Buckle up."

See? She told herself. This is how a rational guy behaves.

"I thought you got sucked out," growled Jack.

I rest my case.

"We going higher, or lower?" she said.

"Going through." Jack gripped the controls, maintaining as much stability as his considerable strength could muster. "Too much traffic."

"Thank you summer vacation."

"What was that you said about a fine night to fly?" Jack slanted her an ironic smile and relief flooded through her. They were back.

She made it to her seat just as the floor gave way and her stomach collided with her esophagus. There went any hope of an early dinner. "A thousand-foot freefall?" Kira asked.

"Fifteen-hundred."

She shook her head.

"You going to help me, or what?"

Kira laughed and grabbed her controls. For the next thirty minutes they played red rover with air currents, often reading each other's directions with a silent glance.

Flying through weather seemed to enhance their camaraderie and Kira thanked heaven they had that distraction tonight. Otherwise, they'd be in the Mile High Club, wondering what the hell to say, and making secret plans to never see each other again.

That simply couldn't happen. Because if Kira had to spend her life wrestling five- hundred-ton bombs on the rim of the stratosphere, the person she most wanted to do it with was Jack.

Never mind why.

Chapter Four

Moral dilemma number four –
Where is the line between teasing and torture?

By the time they shut the plane down, caught the hotel shuttle and checked into their rooms, it was pushing one a.m. Seattle time, four a.m. New York time. Still, the youngsters in the crew were rarin' to go taste some nightlife. Kira just wanted to find Arlo, have a nightcap and gauge the temperature of their future.

The contrast between Jack's incendiary reactions and Arlo's tepid attention confused her. Though she suspected jealousy was his driving force, Jack behaved like a man who was totally, thrillingly into her. Arlo, on the other hand, seemed more mature, more restrained.

Less like a caveman.

She didn't have the experience to decide whether to give up on Arlo completely and look for a rational version of Jack, or continue this snail's pace of a relationship and hope for the best. She desperately needed some time alone with him to discuss it and find out.

Unfortunately, he'd deplaned with the passengers, checked into room three-hundred-thirteen and promptly vaporized into the city, leaving her deflated and petulant. Not to mention exhausted.

Jack, more subdued than usual, had half-heartedly offered to buy her a beer in the hotel lounge, but she had declined, preferring to sulk alone in her room and away from his prehistoric appeal.

Her life as she knew it was over. Flipping open her suitcase, she tossed the romance novel she'd bought at the airport onto the bedside stand, figuring that was all the action she was likely to get tonight, or any other night.

With a sigh, she set out a pathetically small array of cosmetics in the bathroom, peeled the paper lid off a drinking glass and turned down her bed. Reaching for the plastic ice bucket, she decided she might as well go get some now, before changing into her nightie and hitting the sack.

As she opened her door and stepped out into the hushed corridor, she heard the telltale click of a card-key. She spun just in time to see a familiar veil of blonde hair and an obscenely long leg disappear into room three-hundred-thirteen.

Kira marched down the corridor, face heating, and lifted both fists to pound on the door. A giggle from inside almost stopped her. Not quite. She rapped gently, and pushed her chin out as the door swung open.

"Kira!" Arlo's tie hung around his neck like a loose noose and his sand-colored hair was disheveled. Behind him, Svetlana lounged on the bed, her smeared lipstick a testament to *antics interruptus*.

"What's the meaning of this?" Oh God. Let a hole open up and swallow her now. She couldn't believe she actually said that.

"I didn't get the chance to tell you," Arlo stammered. "I was going to, but the turbulence—"

"You had the past two weeks to break up with me, Arlo." Why didn't she feel anything? "Forget it."

Shouldn't she be angry, feel betrayed? "I should've known."

She waved a tired hand and pressed her forehead against a developing headache. To her surprise, Svetlana stood and sauntered over.

"You can't have all the good ones, Kira," she said softly. "You must leave some leftovers for us."

"I'm a leftover?" Arlo said.

"No, no. Not you, darling." She smiled and Arlo smiled back. Kira's stomach heaved.

"What are you talking about?" Kira asked.

Svetlana tossed her hair. "Jack wants you, Arlo wants me. Now we're even." She shrugged and turned away, business finished.

"This isn't a contest," Kira choked. "Jack and I are friends. Not lovers. You're welcome to him." Did her heart just thud against her stomach?

"Tell that to Jack," Svetlana said. "I've tried to get him." And her seductive smile, hidden from Arlo's view by the veil of hair, promised she'd try again.

Arlo cleared his throat. "I've seen how possessive he is of you and I won't compete with him, Kira. Nor will I live in fear of what he might do to me if I fail you somehow."

"But—"

"He's always at your condo when I show up. You might want to ask yourself why you allow him to butt in when your date might expect an intimate evening."

"It's not good form," Svetlana added. As if she needed to. Message received loud and clear.

"Sorry, Kira. Goodbye."

The door closed gently in her face. She raised her fist to rap again and dropped it. What was the use? Arlo'd made his choice and it wasn't Kira. Arguing with him would only result in embarrassment for everyone. Especially her.

Might as well slink back to her room and spend her *Sleepless in Seattle* night figuring out how to exact her revenge on Jack for scaring Arlo off. For scaring all her potential boyfriends off. Somewhere, somehow, he was going to pay.

* * * * *

Jack paid the bartender, stuffed a dollar bill in the tip cup and collected his twenty-ouncer for the trip back upstairs.

Kira'd turned him down for a beer. She never turned him down for a beer, or anything for that matter.

Until Arlo. Jack gave the elevator button an extra-hard punch.

He didn't need more information to realize he was a goner. She'd begun the separation process. Wouldn't be long now.

He recognized the signs. His mother'd done the same thing. First she stopped picking him up after school. Then she stopped being home when he got there. Later and later in the evening she'd return, until finally one night, she didn't.

Women erased you gradually. Unlike men, who simply beat the everloving shit out of you before leaving. Like his father.

Whatever. The result was still the same. They left. And they never came back.

He got off the elevator and stalked down the hallway, glowering at Arlo's room as he passed.

Tinkling female laughter fanned out.

Kira?

Jack froze. The hair on his arms stood up and a flash of white heat behind his eyes nearly blinded him.

Before reason had any hope of returning, he spun and his fist smashed down on the door.

*****

There she came, right on time. Jack sat at a table for two in the hotel restaurant the next morning and watched Kira burst out of the elevator and sway across the lobby.

He took a sip of lukewarm coffee and licked his chops. He'd been right there at the same table most of the night, after assuming the laughter emerging from Arlo's room had come out of Kira's awesome mouth and nearly pounding the door down to get to her.

Would he have killed Arlo over this woman walking toward him right now? Hard to say. If it hadn't turned out to be Svet in Arlo's room, who knows what might have happened.

Jack's sexual possessiveness over Kira didn't make sense to him. Nothing did anymore. He only knew that watching her walk in those tight white shorts, blue tank top that fit like paint and cute little sneakers with the pompom sticking out the back gave him a hard-on the size of Italy.

Arlo claimed to have broken up with her, which proved Jack's theory that Arlo had always been a shithead waiting to happen. No man with half a dick would dump her. Jack intended to throw it righteously in Kira's face, the same way he'd almost delivered Arlo's carcass to her doorstep like a cat gifting its owner with a dead mouse. He had to amuse himself somehow to keep from ravishing her on this whale watch. Trashing Pinhead seemed a good place to start.

"Morning," she said primly.

"Hey." He leaned back and motioned for her to sit down. "Sleep well?"

She murmured noncommittally.

Jack poured her a cup of coffee from the carafe on the table, added two creams and pushed it over in front of her. "Drink up. We've got to be at the dock in forty-five minutes."

She obediently took a sip, put the cup in the saucer, and sighed. He noticed her eyes looked guarded and behind the green glitter of them, lay a jagged shard of resentment.

"Everything okay?"

"Sure. Fine. Why do you ask?" Her chin lifted and her gaze sharpened.

"Ever find Arlo?"

"Yes, I did." She leaned forward, elbows on table, and he automatically copied her posture.

"When's the wedding?" he asked. This was going to be enlightening.

She leaned back. "I'm thinking autumn. I always wanted a colorful wedding."

Liar. His heart skipped a beat. As far as he knew, she'd always been truthful. Suddenly all the fun got sucked out of his day. "So soon?" he said to buy time.

What was going on here? Had Arlo lied? Because if he had…

Over Kira's shoulder Jack spied the happy couple in the lobby. Public fondling. No furtive, guilty glances to see who might be watching. They had nothing to hide.

His gaze shot to Kira. She babbled on about the wedding, providing the fanciful details a three-year-old might create. He noticed she didn't quite meet his eyes.

Busted.

About to confront her, he changed his mind. This could be a laugh-and-a-half. She had something up her sleeve and he suddenly found himself enthralled. Learned something new everyday. Even about your best bud.

* * * * *

Within an hour they pulled into the Marina in Everett. The summer day had dawned with rare glory, cloudless and so clear, Kira had seen Mt. Ranier towering in the distance as they'd swooped up I-5. Once again, Jack had fallen into an oddly contemplative mood. She'd expected him to go ballistic over the fictional wedding and had planned on playing it to the hilt, driving him over the edge and into the sack.

What a washout.

All through the night she'd moped about her dismal prospects and had decided that if Arlo had rejected her because of Jack's alleged feelings for her, then others probably had too. She supposed she'd enabled Jack by allowing him to come and go in her condo as he pleased and by permitting him more of a say in her life than she should've. It'd been easier for her to submit to some of his insane demands than to fight him. Not that she didn't fight. She'd merely chosen her battles carefully. Too carefully. He'd developed a sense of entitlement over her, which could be resolved one of two ways. The way she saw it she could either battle to the death for her sexual freedom, or make him pony up and take care of her needs. Right now he controlled her without having to lift a finger for her sexually or get ensnared in a monogamous relationship. Meanwhile she was a ticking time bomb of lust. If she didn't have an orgasm provided by someone other than herself pretty soon, she was going to freak out.

Now, he sat there in the driver's seat, content, happy and safe in his comfort zone. While she imploded with need, still imagining his erection between her legs and wanting him more than air. If Jack could have his cake and eat it too, so could she. And he was the ticket. Time to shake him up a little. He'd certainly throttled her. Forget the 'friends' thing. They'd survive. And if she had to deal with his angst on a day-to-day basis anyway, she might as well get an orgasm or two hundred out of it.

It was the perfect situation. She just needed to convince him. But how?

Jack slid into a parking spot. Outside the rental car, they paused to put on sunglasses. Jack hooked an arm around her shoulders and they walked to the docks.

"You want more coffee? I want coffee. There's a shop over there." Kira pointed to a blue clapboard snack shop nestled amongst a cluster of outfitters, restaurants and ticket offices.

Jack took her finger and folded it back into her palm. "Everything we need is on the boat." He shot a glance at his watch. "We'd better get a move on."

They approached the wharf, where multiple ferries rolled at anchor and young families lined up to board. All the gates were closed, however, and Kira noticed they still had fifteen minutes to spare until departure time.

She really needed more caffeine to sharpen her plotting skills. Besides, they were in Seattle, the coffee capital of the free world. It seemed sinful to *not* indulge. "Jack, we have time—"

"This way. He took her elbow as she veered back toward the coffee shop, steering her down the quay in the opposite direction.

She glanced over her shoulder. "We're not going on one of those ferries?"

"Nope." He stopped in front of a sleek, modern cabin cruiser that had been outfitted with an enclosed observation deck over the cockpit. "I chartered a private boat. To celebrate our first flight together."

His thoughtfulness nearly undid her. And almost repaid the debt she felt he owed her for interfering with Arlo. Maybe it wasn't entirely Jack's fault, but he'd played a major role. If, like Svet implied, Jack wanted Kira for himself, so be it. She'd let him have her.

But not quite.

"We have this all to ourselves?" The seeds of a plan took root in her mind.

Jack nodded and grinned. "Just you, me and the orcas."

"And the captain and crew," Kira added slyly as a crisply uniformed steward handed her aboard.

"They won't bother us."

The roots of the idea fanned out.

After greeting the captain, Jack guided her up a set of metal spiral stairs to the enclosure on top. When he opened the door, Kira sucked in a breath.

Bronze leather sofas wrapped around the sparkling glass and chrome perimeter. As she stepped inside, her feet sank into plush chocolate brown carpeting. The savory aroma of crusty rolls, croissants and coffee seeped into her nostrils, making her mouth water as she searched for the source.

There it was. To her left sat a linen covered table loaded with fresh fruit and baked goods. Kira wandered over and inspected the tasty treats before selecting a donut. "Jack," she sighed, licking the glaze. "This is spectacular."

Baskets of peonies were placed at elegant intervals amongst the furnishings and she knew immediately they were special order. For one thing, they were her favorite flower and Jack knew it. For another, a prominent, congratulatory sign was draped around one of the pots.

Did he feel subconscious guilt for ruining her love life?

She became aware of music playing softly on the sound system and when she turned in a daze, she noted a balcony, to view the whales al fresco.

The ideal setting for making a deal.

With her back to him, she composed her mouth into a dazzling smile, licked her lips and widened her eyes until they hurt. She spun around with extra oomph, tossing her hair so it flung over one shoulder.

Jack had been investigating her ass. With a man's expertise, he blinked and flashed his gaze to her face. Their eyes met and held and something in his flickered out to greet her.

Baby. Come to Momma.

Kira sauntered across the room, directing her hands to frame and caress her hips. She felt like an idiot. But it had the intended effect. Men were so easy to please.

"Let's talk about that kiss," she said, stopping in front of him and placing a hand on his chest. Jack's face closed down.

"What about it?" he asked warily.

"I thought it was spectacular," she cooed. "I'd like to try it again. To make sure."

His eyes narrowed and he took a step back, turning to inspect the pastries. "What about Arlo?"

She'd forgotten that part.

"Didn't bother you last night," she tried.

"Does now." He popped a donut hole into his mouth.

Crapola. Now she'd have to admit the lie or he'd think she was a slut.

So much for spinning a seductive mood. Kira dropped the stripper act. "I lied. I broke up with him." Okay, so she lied again but she had her pride!

"Why lie about it?" He sounded casual. Kira wasn't fooled. Every muscle in his body seemed coiled to strike. Man did she want some of that.

"Because I wanted you to get jealous enough to kiss me again." The admission sucked so much energy out of her she had to grip the edge of the table.

Underfoot, the boat's engines roared. The wharf slanted away as they turned and headed out into Puget Sound.

Again, his voice sounded steady, almost lazy. "What makes you think I kissed you out of jealousy?"

Kicking someone in the nuts never sounded so attractive.

"This is ridiculous!" she bellowed.

His head snapped around. "What's wrong?"

Interesting. He was jumpy. Maybe not so cavalier after all. "Everything, Jack."

His jaw clenched and she knew he knew what she was thinking. "Why am I afraid of what you're going to say next?"

"There's nothing to be afraid of. It's just me."

He snorted.

"I'm the same person I was before the kiss."

"Who do you think you're talking to?"

A big sphincter, "Not sure anymore. The Jack I know wouldn't shy from conversation. We've always been able to talk about everything. Why not now?"

* * * * *

Because talking is what got us into this mess. Looking back, Jack realized talking used to prevent him from jumping her bones. He'd get so wrapped up in a conversation with Kira, he'd forget everything else. Unfortunately, that had changed.

Now, talking to her made him so horny he wanted to lick the words right out of her sassy mouth. There didn't seem to be anything he could do to quench his desire, except leave. And he couldn't do that. He'd made that damn promise to Tom.

Take care of her.

Yeah right. He'd take care of her all right. In bed. He'd be happy to accommodate, but he didn't think that was quite what Tom meant.

Then again, everything was open to interpretation. He'd have to think about that.

Against his better judgment they were speeding headfirst into fuckfestville and he was running out of ideas to prevent it. He didn't *want* to prevent it anymore.

Too bad he couldn't fast-forward to the inevitable. He knew it was only a matter of time before she left him. He'd already been made aware of his particular flaw and was awaiting the day when his over-protectiveness would smother her and she'd hand him a one-way ticket out.

Whoa.

Wait a minute.

Why hadn't he thought of this before?

He could smother her. Plenty of women had driven *him* away by smothering. It worked every time.

All he had to do was be himself.

They'd get back to New York, she'd dump him and he'd be free, but with the added bonus of having had her in every way possible, first.

His promise to Tom would be fulfilled and even Mike couldn't kill him because the hookup would be Kira's idea. Everything would be Kira's idea. From start-up to breakup. Jack wouldn't lift a finger.

It was the perfect plan—airtight and foolproof.

Slowly, he turned toward her. "What do you want to talk about?"

Kira stared at him. Her eyes were huge and dark and that lower lip still looked used and bruised from their kiss. *Just wait 'til I finish with you.*

"We've grown too comfortable, gotten used to each other."

She hadn't remembered to wear a T-shirt bra and if he tilted his head just so, he could catch the peak of a nipple.

"We're taking each other for granted."

Salty sea air dampened her skin, softening her edges and making her dewy. He wondered how she'd look after he made her stupid, spent and wobbly in his arms. He'd be finding that out real soon. Yes sir.

"Jack."

Just as soon as they got back to the hotel. He'd rip off those shorts, throw her on the bed…

"Are you listening?"

Those long legs would spread wide and surround him, he'd sink inside her…

"Forget it." Kira turned away.

"Okay." He shrugged. *Three, two, one.*

"Jack."

"Hmmm?" He ambled over to a rack of magazines on the wall and pretended to study them. She followed, resting a knee on the leather sofa and studying his profile.

"We spend all this time together. It's stupid that we're not already lovers."

He said nothing, pressing a finger to his lips to keep from biting her.

"We're going to be flying together all the time. Think of the layovers."

Oh, I'm thinking of the layovers. "Isn't this rather sudden?"

"We've known each other fifteen years." Kira's hands gripped the sofa back, but one finger broke free and rapidly tapped the cushioned frame. Jack had a momentary spurt of sympathy. This had to be hard for her—he'd never have brought it up. But knowing precisely how he'd make it up to her later enabled him to let the torture continue.

"I'm not sure it's a good idea." He almost gacked on the words.

"Why not?"

He tried to inject compassion into his tone, but it came out sounding more pompous than he intended. "We've gotten along fine without sex until now."

Kira made a face. "Who's gotten along fine?"

Good point. "Why ask for trouble?"

"Maybe there wouldn't be any trouble."

He raised his eyebrows.

"What if we had an agreement?"

This was getting better and better. "What kind of agreement?"

Kira licked her lips and drew a deep breath, hitching her breasts so high Jack almost got a nosebleed. "We can do layovers."

"What?" Jack's bark was genuine.

Her fingers braided. "Well, you don't want a relationship and I'm free at the moment. We're obviously attracted to each other. When we're on trips, it can be a fantasy. For both of us."

Jack's jaw dropped, but the rest of him was paralyzed with astonishment. "What happens when we get home?"

Kira shrugged. "Business as usual."

"That's sick!"

"No it's not. Listen."

"I don't want to listen! I can't believe you think I'd do that."

"Jack—"

"Don't *Jack* me. Have you made this deal with anyone else?"

"N-no."

"What a relief." He smacked the wall. "I'm honored to be the only layover in your life." *But you might not be if you say no.*

Kira dropped her face into her hands. "This is coming out all wrong."

"I certainly hope so," Jack fumed. He couldn't believe this. What did she think he was, her fuck buddy?

"What I mean is, when we're away, as long as we're not committed to anyone else, sex can be a part of our life together. No strings. We just tell each other if one of us starts sleeping with someone else."

"I'd never sleep with someone else while I was with you."

"Good," she nodded. "Neither would I. But if one of us meets someone, we should give two weeks' notice."

"That's all?" he spewed.

"Three weeks', then."

"This isn't a job! Okay. Okay." Jack leaned back and scraped his face. Breathe, Grayson. Breathe. This isn't the first time someone offered casual sex. It's just the first offer from Kira, your best friend, your frickin' responsibility. "You're telling me you'll make my wildest fantasies come true and be my pal. But when some other sucker trots down the pike you'll say 'See ya'."

"I like the part about wild fantasies. That's good."

"Thanks. I thought of it myself."

They got silent for a moment.

"Well anyway, yes," Kira said. "And you're free to say 's'long' at any time too."

"No explanations, no apologies?" No, 'Jack don't leave me I need you'?

"Exactly."

How do you like that? He was expendable. Temporary. Jack glared out over the water. To be fair, he always figured Kira spent so much time with him because she had nothing better to do and no one better to do it with. But to hear her actually say it blew out his solar plexus.

Why? It's what he wanted, what he himself planned—only a helluva lot better. He had to hand it to her.

"We'll always be friends," she said.

He scowled.

"I mean, when it's over, we'll go back to the way we've always been."

"Like we are now?" Impossible. People couldn't sleep together, break up and be friends. What he was facing here was the death of his relationship with Kira, the demise of the purest friendship he'd ever known.

But with some really cosmic sex first.

Hard to weigh out.

Who was he kidding? It was over already. He'd ended it with the kiss and she'd hammered the coffin lid with her proposal. Now they saw each other as sex objects and could never, ever revert to platonic.

Might as well go for it. "One more question. Why only layovers?"

Kira set free the wide, sweet smile that never failed to calcify his cock. "Because it won't seem icky, like Jack and Kira."

He had to ask. Kira wanted anonymous, stranger sex. Not sex with Jack Grayson, her icky friend. Great. How could something be worse and better at the same time? Jack's head was about to explode.

He flexed his shoulders and rolled his neck. Kira got up and moved behind him, massaging the sore muscles with familiar, comforting hands.

"What do you say?" she whispered in his ear.

Lust dripped down his spine and splattered all over his groin. "I say we're going to regret this."

"I don't think so, Jack."

He snatched her hand and brought it round to his lips. Dread poked at his heart but he shoved it back as he flicked his tongue between her fingers and she puddled against his back.

"We'll do layovers."

Chapter Five

Moral dilemma number five –
When you assume, do you really make an ass out of me, or just you?

"Starting tonight," he added.

"Why wait?" she purred.

He turned and lunged for her and they fell onto the couch in a tangle of limbs.

In the corners of her mind, Kira had harbored a notion that their first time would be awkward, funny, a hoot-and-a-half. But Jack looked deadly serious. His glittering eyes scanned her face while he slowly moved an exploratory hand up her waist to her breast—as if testing to make sure this was for real, that she'd let him touch her. At her slight nod, he leaned over and followed the trail with his lips.

His other hand inched up beneath her tank top, gathered the fabric and pulled it off over her head. He disposed of that on the floor and went for her shorts, yanking the button free.

Kira fumbled with his clothing while he kicked off his shoes and quick as a wink, the feel of his warm, nearly naked body pressing her down into the cushions shocked the shit out of her.

"You're killing me," he murmured. And he sucked her nipple into his mouth, teasing it tenderly with his teeth and the firm tip of his hot, lapping tongue.

Killing *him*? Kira writhed breathlessly beneath him.

His rigid cock pressed into her abdomen, making her vision fog as a swollen, billowing need infused her blood. She was about to have sex with Jack! Sex. With Jack. Something she'd only ever thought about with objective curiosity sat poised to become a most subjective investigation. Had she gone crazy? Perhaps. Would she regret it? Maybe. As his warm flesh imprinted hers and pushed her down further into the cushions she lost her ability to care about later.

Opening her legs, she cradled his hips between them, rocking gently and savoring the raw freshness of being with him this way. Rumors around Pan Air held that he excelled at sex, though as far as she knew, she'd never run into anyone who'd actually had it with him. Until now.

"I don't know what to do first," he whispered in a voice thick with arousal. A voice she'd never heard but suddenly and keenly knew she'd always yearned to. "I want all of you at once. Tell me what you want me to do."

She had a choice?

Kira licked her lips and he opened his mouth and sucked them and her tongue inside. She opened hers and they devoured each other, hands everywhere, melding and fusing, his skin hot and silky, sliding over her body. *Jack.* His fingers hooking her panties and sliding them down, her hands pushing his briefs off, clenching his tight, muscular ass.

"Tell me what to do."

Before she could answer he drew long, feather-light fingers up her leg and toyed with her labia. He fondled her slowly with his palm, spreading her creamy juices around her inner thighs and watching her face intently. A small part of her registered that this was Jack—with his familiar scent and beloved face—but in truth, the closer he advanced the more like a stranger he became. The realization both alarmed and intrigued her, exciting her beyond what she would've considered normal yesterday. They were both at a threshold, a place where they'd have stopped to talk and analyze in a more sensible past. Kira had a vague idea of asking him if he was certain he wanted to go down this road, if for no other reason than to make sure of her own certainty, when two of his fingers plunged into her pussy.

Her lungs ballooned in her chest.

Never, ever would she have reckoned on Jack's fingers in there. And that was just his fingers! Gasping for breath she wondered how she'd survive the onslaught of his cock.

Of him.

Should she get it over with now and die a quick and pleasurable death? Or delay the inevitable and let him torture her into an early grave.

"Get inside me, now."

Jack slid upright, slipping hands over her stomach, darkened eyes worshipping every inch of her flesh. "You're sure that's what you want? No warmup?"

"Stop second-guessing what I want!" she said. "You do it all the time and—"

"Okay, okay. Relax." He chuckled—another low, sexy sound she'd never heard before. The vibration of it through her stomach telegraphed straight into her clit. Her pussy wept with need. "Have it your way," he said. "But put this on me first."

That stinker!

From somewhere he produced a condom and she

dove under him to unroll it. Later she'd ask how he'd gotten one but for now…

Fully erect, he was magnificent and she couldn't resist a little friendly exploration before covering him with latex. As she ran her teeth along the rigid rim of his baby-soft head, he shuddered against her cheek and placed trembling hands on her shoulders. Kira distracted him momentarily by swirling her fingernails along the outside of his fuzzy thighs, then, curving her tongue around the bottom of his shaft, she tightened her upper lip and sucked him inside so abruptly he almost launched off the couch. She would've continued the delicate torture—wanted to hear him shout her name and shudder with the unbearable ecstasy she provided—but with a groan, he pushed her gently away. "Not now, not yet. I won't be able to stop."

"Then don't. Let me do this."

"No." Another groan that came out suspiciously like a whimper. "You first."

Such a characteristic response, even in the throes of lust. It pleased her beyond measure that his considerate behavior toward her would extend between the sheets. She could always count on Jack to take the noble road.

Surrendering to his simple, unselfish demand, she secured the condom and lay back. "Later then. I want to do everything with you, Jack. Everything."

He dropped over her and spread her legs with his knees. "But this first," he said.

"Yes."

He plunged hard and deep, finding the end of her, making her gasp with the fullness of his body and how easily he fit. As if they'd been poured into the opposite sides of the same mold.

"Jack?" He slid out, in, out, moving with slow, insistent strokes. Kira's hips rose, pulling him deeper with each lunge and he began thrusting smoothly and gracefully like a well-oiled piston.

The sense of familiarity coupled with the excitement of being with someone new began to get to her.

A freshet of urgency spurted through her, intensifying as it took control and gobbled the edges of her mind.

He had her head in his hands, hot eyes on her face. "I'm inside you." There was wonder in his voice. "Oh Kira, this is good."

"You feel wonderful."

"So do you." He sounded pleasantly surprised, as if his expectations had been met and exceeded. It made her want to do more, *be* more for him. "We've got to slow down. I'm going to lose it."

"Then lose it," she said. *Go crazy, for me, in me, because of me. Go over the edge Jack. I want to drive you insane.* Jack rarely let her do anything for him. At last here was something—

"Not yet."

Every cell in her body screamed in outrage when he kicked the tempo back a notch, breathing easier and lifting his weight off her, but staying inside. He reared back on his knees perpendicular to her, gripped her bottom and pushed himself in as far as possible. Then he lifted her hips and started circling them gently around his shaft.

Low frequency vibrations surged through her, exploding in her abdomen, legs and everywhere. Her back arched as if zapped with fifty thousand volts and she flung out her arms, gripping the cushions and gritting her teeth as a thirty decibel moan nearly tore out her throat.

"You have eight thousand nerve endings and I'm going to make each one sing," he said.

Every centimeter of him rubbed every centimeter of her, creating agonizingly intense friction in her super-sensitized vagina and provoking a shattering awareness of his body possessing hers.

At his first sexual touch he'd stuck a toe over her last line of defense. Now he'd been unleashed to infiltrate every aspect of her life, her body and her manicured emotions. She hadn't reckoned on relinquishing that power and handing it to him on a platter, on having nothing in reserve, nothing to fall back on. But she could feel the last shreds of control seeping out behind each of his thrusts. Did it matter? She could trust him. He was her best friend.

"This would work better with a ribbed condom," he said thickly and started moving faster.

"It can't be better than this," she gasped. Nothing could top having him inside her.

"Every time is going to be better, Kira." The building strain in his voice turned her on. He was holding back, pleasuring her first, tending her needs the same way he did out of bed. "When we're over, you'll remember me as the best you've ever had."

When they were over. Right now she couldn't envision the end, even though she knew it would come. Right now all she could think of was Jack, the mind-blowing sensations he aroused in every aspect of her being, his elemental scent and passion-drugged eyes.

"Now do me," he ordered.

Kira braced her feet on either side of him and began rotating. Jack groaned, leaning back on his hands and closing his eyes as his body began to quake between her legs. "Faster."

She obliged and everything blew up. He fell onto her, pumping madly, ramming her high on the pillows as his hips pounded her. Her brain went white as she cried out and gripped him, coming in great, heaving waves, thrashing and begging, unable to withstand the shocks jolting her entire being.

Then he came with a racking, guttural shout, calling her name in the way she had envisioned, yet sounding different than she ever could've guessed. Her name had a power on his tongue that it lacked on others—as if bursting like magma from a long dormant volcano. With her last brain cell disengaged by unending orgasm, she lacked the capacity to properly analyze it. All she knew, as she rose into an oblivion of bliss, was that she needed to hear him cry out for her like that again. And again.

They clung to each other, damp and quivering as his thrusts slowed and stopped. She spasmed around him, and each time, he let out a growl, kissing her neck, kneading her breast, while she kept him in a leg-lock. A reluctance to let go and acknowledge the end of a first to cap all firsts tightened her grip. She thought back to her first solo flight and the exhilaration of utter self-reliance, utter confidence and sweeping joy it had given her. The cascade of emotions as she came down from this particular high rioted through her system so violently she feared it would wash out of her eyes in a torrent of tears. She rammed her face into his shoulder and clung, deciding to let him speak first so she could follow his lead into this uncharted territory.

Certainly any day now he'd have something to say. He usually did. He rolled onto his back, swinging Kira around so she lay on top. She settled against his chest, nuzzling into his warm thicket of hair and tucking her limbs cozily beneath his solid, reassuring weight.

"I always knew there was a good reason to be friends with you," he finally said shakily. His fettered tone hinted at a deeper level of feeling and nearly undid her with a desire for more, but she drew a breath, moderated her own tone and replied, "You got the payoff today. All those years of hard work."

* * * * *

"Makes it all worthwhile," Jack said. She'd shattered his expectations, his little pal, and he kicked himself for not getting here sooner. She lay over him, all arms and legs, warm and silky and sweet smelling—the best layover he'd ever had. The only one he'd had in months.

It'd been forever since he bothered looking at another woman. Kira had slowly infected him. And why not? She was a babe to end all babes. It was about time they hooked up and he felt sure she'd stick to the deal. No worries of Kira doing an about-face and demanding more. She was the Queen of Disposable Men.

This was great. Exactly what they both needed. Kira could date at home and have him on the side. She'd settle in with someone, or get tired of him and he'd be free. But he'd have the satisfaction of knowing she'd remember him the rest of her life.

For a second, the thought of her leaving hollowed him out like a gutted deer, but he shook it off.

"How was I?" Kira's question broke into his thoughts.

He squeezed her, noting how smoothly she fit against him, how oddly comfortable he felt despite this being their first time. A tiny alarm clanged in the recesses of his brain. Usually that signaled retreat time. Lazy and strangely replete, he was in no particular rush. Why? Must be because he'd never fucked a good friend before. "You have to ask? You almost killed me."

"It's nice to hear the words."

Amazing. With anyone else, he'd be itching to leave for sure. He was so glad they did this. "Honey, the earth moved. You're the best." If she only knew—

She slapped him. "Not those words. Yuck."

"You were a delicate blossom, unfurling in my heart." Corny, but curiously true.

"Stop."

Did she not appreciate his romantic side? "Actually, I can't wait to blow this ice cream stand."

She snuggled in closer, causing a rush of bliss to charge through his nervous system. "That's more like it."

"Going to get up, shake it dry and leave."

"Even better."

Cool. She wanted fun and games. While he could've been coaxed into indulging her with rainbows and lollipops and *might* have been induced into admitting how totally she'd rocked his world, he was on more familiar ground with the wisecracks. She really was easy to be with. "Too bad I'm stuck for another day."

Kira lifted her face and those green eyes knocked him into the middle of next week. "Think you're up for it?"

Jack grinned, cupping her lush little ass and bearing down. "Will be, soon."

"Not soon enough," she said.

"Are you implying I'm not worthy?"

He felt her shrug. "I didn't say that."

Even though he knew she was joking—that this was the way they always communicated—fear squeezed his chest. "I'm not a teenager. It might take thirty minutes."

"S'ok."

She expected more. Damn. He'd taken too long at the draw. Should've had her in the back of his Camaro ten years ago when he'd had more staying power. Now he had *lightweight* stamped on his forehead. "Is that a challenge?"

"Jack, I was teasing. Geez. Like you're really going to shake it dry and leave? Relax. It's just me."

Not anymore. After mind-bending sex she was no longer ordinary Kira. Now she was his sex-goddess. His Towering Pillar of Lust.

"I'll wait." She sighed.

He had to keep her happy or she'd leave. Crap. What had he gotten himself into? Wait, he wanted her to leave, right? Yeah. He did. So, would lousy sex send her packing?

That idea curled in and back out in maybe ten seconds.

Lousy sex might get rid of her faster but he had a reputation to maintain. Besides, he wanted her to remember him and get hot. Not roll her eyes. "No need to wait."

Her head came up and a gleam entered those gorgeous eyes. In one swift motion he had her on her back, his tongue gliding down soft, sex-warmed flesh. Securing a nipple in one hand, he spread her legs again and inspected that hot, slippery haven where he'd reached Nirvana.

At first lick, her back arched and she gripped his head. He tortured her slowly, flicking, tasting, testing to see what incited the most explosive reaction, then he went at it with the hunger and lust that'd been building since he'd met her.

At thirteen she hadn't exactly been every teenage boy's wet dream. He remembered her as gangly and coltish, a plain-Jane tomboy. Oddly enough, she'd calmed him and made him horny as hell at the same time. Lust for Kira had always knocked around in his rib cage.

Finally he was living the dream and though the experience had proved far more awesome than he ever could've imagined, soon it would cease to control him. If his past experience with women was anything to go by, in no time flat he'd be over her. Hitting the highway.

Free forever.

Had to send up a special prayer of thanks for that. Because otherwise the lust might have pinned itself to his ass and followed him around for all eternity.

And what lust it was. Her spicy flavor on his tongue and aroused scent in his nostrils ignited the ember he'd carried around in his dick for an eon. If it hadn't been for Mike and Tom, he'd have immolated himself on her pyre long ago. Sucking ravenously at her labia and lapping her clit at expertly timed intervals, he wondered where they'd be now if he had. Would they have taken the conventional route and gotten married? Had kids? Whoa! Roadblock. He eased around the sawhorse and drew in a breath.

The idea didn't scare the crap out of him like he'd expected it to. Maybe the security of a binding union could be nice—if any woman could put up with him that long. Could Kira?

His tongue hesitated a microsecond and rested heavily on her clit. She mewed and lunged desperately against his face so he picked up the pace. Hot damn she was loud. And wiggly. He had to grab her thighs and sway to her beat just to stay on board. Shit! Who knew her fingers were so strong? Might lose a few hairs.

He grinned against her pussy.

Work it Grayson. Work it. Make her beg for you. Make her plead for you.

Make her grieve for you when you're gone.

*****

So they'd done the horizontal hula.

Kira inspected herself in the bathroom mirror for physical evidence of what had happened in her soul. She looked exactly the same, except for one or two bite marks. But the lightness inside her body made her question what she was seeing in the mirror.

She'd expected to be a-twitter with nervous energy, fretting about her less-than-ideal butt, worried that she'd look weird in the throes of passion.

Like any other woman she'd always been worried her body or her lovemaking would be disappointing. Somehow Jack had obliterated those worries without any obvious effort. Her physical insecurities had vaporized and she couldn't figure out why. Pinning down what was different with Jack wasn't going to be easy. He annoyed the hell out of her for one thing, for another, she couldn't wait to get back to him.

"Get out here!" His voice boomed through the door.

She opened it and met his gaze, sauntering over to sit on his lap. "How did you hear about this cruise?" An eye-popping array of colorful condoms shamelessly displayed in the bathroom had hinted that this was no ordinary charter. She didn't want to know if someone like Svetlana had sampled it with Jack. But she couldn't seem to stop herself from asking.

"Lea mentioned it a few months ago."

That figured. "Have you done this before?" Now why did she go and ask that? She didn't want to hear an affirmative so she glued on a big smile and nipped his chin. "Joking."

"Yeah, I take all my girls whale watching."

Cool. It was his first time too. Kira melted over him, feeling cherished and unique—if that made any sense, considering she wasn't. The feeling gave her an idea. "Let's make an addendum to the layover deal."

Underneath her, Jack tensed and stopped stroking her back. "We just got started and already you want changes?"

"Only a little one."

"What sort of addendum?" he asked cautiously, fingers kneading as if they wanted to continue stroking her but had been leashed. Geez. Did he have to be so wary all the time?

"We can't recycle dates on layovers."

"And that means?"

"When we go out somewhere, it has to be the first time for both of us."

He relaxed again. "Honey, with you, everything feels like the first time."

Okay, his reply was sarcastic, flip. The usual. But he'd probably comply.

She didn't know why she wanted it this way, but she did. Something inside her demanded that Jack see his time with her as unique. After all, this was a fantasy and as such, she could dream.

"We didn't have slow sex yet," he muttered, hand tracing the line of her spine, sliding up and around seeking secret, soft spaces.

"Give it some time," Kira said with a butt wiggle against his burgeoning erection. She flattened her palms across his hard pecs, leaning on him and admiring his solid physique. "I wanted it, but noooo."

He grabbed a breast in each hand and flicked her nipples with his thumbs. Her back arched and she gasped at the surprise attack.

"You're insatiable," he accused.

"Is that a complaint?"

"No." His eyes closed as he dropped his hands to her waist, kneading her flesh and pressing her hips into his. "I like you insatiable. We're a good match that way."

But she was only insatiable with Jack. With others, she could take sex or leave it. Preferring, most of the time, to leave it. What made Jack different?

Jack slid down on his back and nestled into the cushions, pulling her along for the ride. She propped her elbows on his chest, resting her chin in a hand and gazing into his eyes. What made Jack so irresistible she was willing to risk years of friendship, just to have him in bed?

"Stop staring and go pick your pleasure in the bathroom. I need to be inside you."

"Later," Kira said, gliding to the floor and onto her knees beside him. "I want to taste you first." In truth, she wanted to give back a measure of the soul scrunching pleasure he'd given her a while ago.

Jack groaned. "Get a condom anyway. I like having options."

Kira sighed dramatically but hoisted herself up and trotted into the bathroom. Once again, the dazzling assortment of sex toys greeted her—way too many for the six hours they'd be at sea. She rummaged through the basket and read the package of one interesting-looking prospect—extra rib-o-matic with peppermint enhancement. Sounded good to her.

Placing the treasure between her teeth, she sashayed toward Jack and leaned over. He took it with his teeth then held it up between two fingers to squint at the label.

"Well, if you're determined to kill yourself, may as well make sure you go out in a blaze of glory."

"Might taste good, too."

He brightened. "That, we have to try. I wonder how it makes *you* taste."

"My turn to do you. This time, it's *au natural*."

"If you insist."

Kira massaged his tight, straining erection and slid her chest over it while licking a path along his stomach. His cock fit perfectly between her naked breasts and she bunched them around it, moving back and forth while he closed his eyes and sucked air in pleasure.

"Feel good?" she cooed, and sheathed him with her mouth.

"Damn," he choked, fingers in her hair, hands gripping her face. Kira licked her palm and slid it up and down his shaft, keeping the tip in her mouth while circumnavigating the head with her tongue. "Kira."

"You like this?" she asked, and lapped down his full length. She stopped at his balls and took a taste test, sucking one gingerly into her mouth out of curiosity and delighting in his increasingly frantic sounds.

"Like a water balloon dipped in dental floss," she quipped, kissing her way up his cock again and pulling him fully inside her lips.

"Can't take much more," he gasped but his hands said *stay* so she increased the tempo of her hand and the pressure of her lips. Jack pushed against her mouth, his penis buried in her while she sucked unmercifully.

He felt so good in there, silky and warm and his elemental scent filled her nostrils. She wanted to torture him over the edge.

Suddenly, he thrashed upright and pushed her away. "Get this on quickly."

"But I wanted to—" Unreal. For the second time he'd refused her access—had to be the only man on the planet capable of stopping a blowjob mid-suckle! She didn't think she was *that* lousy, so it had to be some other reason. Yet another new, unfathomable side of Jack to puzzle over.

"Now."

"Have it your way." Far be it from her to analyze an obviously crazy man when peppermint possibilities were coming down the pike. She ripped open the condom and rolled it over him. He pulled her onto his lap and plunged into her.

A tingling sensation erupted in her vagina, sensitizing her flesh for his thrusts. The ribbing drove her insane with pleasure and, already turned on by the foreplay, she shattered in orgasm almost instantaneously with Jack.

"This is unbelievable," she offered on a pant. "I mean I knew we'd be good together, but this goes above and beyond."

Jack's sweat-dampened body undulated as he thrust one final time. "It's *all right,*" he said then quivered.

Kira smacked his chest, too spent to feel outraged, and knowing from his reaction it was more than merely "all right". "Can't you give me anything?"

"I already gave you everything I've got."

No he didn't. So what else was new? Why make an issue of it now?

She reminded herself to enjoy the skin-to-skin contact and the unvarnished freedom from physical insecurities. If there were emotional insecurities down the road, she'd just have to do what she always did. Ignore them. Hey. Worked before.

They snuggled together and basked in the sun streaming in through clear windows. Though central air had taken its toll and seeped into her bones, the sun on her back and Jack's simmering warmth underneath sheltered her in a cozy cocoon she felt reluctant to leave.

After a few minutes, Jack began to twitch, scratch his nose and sigh intermittently, as if impatient to move along. Maybe the sex had recharged some internal battery. Or, more likely, made him want to run. She glanced at him as he slid out from under her and straightened to dress. "S'up?"

"Let's go outside," he said.

Seemed he could deliver afterglow, but only for a prescribed length of time. Kira felt a disturbing dissatisfaction. She chided herself. He wasn't acting out of character. She just supposed some part of her wanted to make him relax, to be a calming influence.

To make him want to stay.

"I hear there's whales in them thar hills," she joked but her voice sounded jacketed in disappointment. No sense wasting time on a pipe dream. She hopped to her feet and finished dressing in a flash, almost beating Jack.

Mimicking his restlessness—or possibly absorbing it and making it her own—she yanked him onto the balcony, and turned her face into the breeze. Jack settled behind, wrapping her in strong arms as they leaned on the railing. She pulled back and watched his profile, the wind ruffling his hair. He had such classically etched features, so physically perfect. And as wild as the sea.

She wondered again why he'd never felt free. The Jack she knew was as footloose as they came, except for his devotion to her and her family. Something had changed. Something subtle, and if she didn't know him so well she might've missed it. But now that she was looking, she saw his humor seemed strained. His teasing had an edge. Also, he wasn't allowing himself to lose control during sex, yet he encouraged her to do so at every opportunity.

What are you afraid of, Jack Grayson? she wondered, surprised again at the word *afraid*. It wasn't an emotion she'd have attributed to Jack. So why did it pop into her head twice in less than a day?

The loudspeaker crackled. "Orcas at three o'clock."

Kira lunged to the other side of the balcony in time to see a majestic black and white shape breach and land with a thundering splash.

"Whoa!" Jack cried. "Will you look at that?"

Tears sprang into her eyes. "I'm speechless," she croaked. A head rush similar to what she experienced upon takeoff made her grip the railing to stay upright.

"Not an easy feat to accomplish." Jack's voice cracked.

The awesome display continued while the captain outlined facts about the pod and how many orcas were in residence. Kira counted three calves, frolicking alongside their mothers.

"I've never seen anything like it." She sucked in an emotional breath as Jack slipped a hand around her waist. Goose bumps decorated her arms while the magnificent animals frolicked in the sparkling water, under the bright sun, dorsal fins towering, tails pounding.

After a few minutes, a mother and child broke away from the pod to investigate the boat. They spy hopped from a short distance, as if extending an invitation to play, and the baby whistled, making an aunt, or an older sibling come rocketing over. "So many families," Kira whispered. "They seem so close."

"Until the boys get kicked out."

At the bitterness in his tone, she shot him a glance and his jaw tightened. "That's the way most of nature works," she answered faintly, unsure of what to say. They'd never talked about his mother and her reasons for doing what she did. Kira'd always assumed Jack had come to terms with it long ago. Apparently she'd been wrong.

"That's what they say," Jack said. Then he blinked and rolled his neck and his demeanor shifted as two whales lifted out of the water at once.

"I wonder what would happen if I jumped in with them," she mused out loud, the adventurer in her tempted sorely. But she was far too smart to take such a risk.

"Might be dangerous."

Leave it to Jack to take her seriously. He could be such a dumbass sometimes. "Might be fun," she taunted.

Jack's grip on her waist tightened. He turned her to face him and pulled her close. "No need for that. We can have just as much fun right here."

She glanced up to meet feverish eyes and thought she surprised a hint of desperation before his mouth came crashing down.

At his plunder, a sonic boom tore through her veins. In seconds he stripped off her shirt and shorts, hiked her legs around his waist and carried her inside.

"Face the window." He bent her forward over the inner railing and dropped his pants, thrusting into her from behind with a possession so fierce, she felt like a wild animal mating in the open. Pushing backwards off the railing and bracing herself against it with her hands, she dropped her face between her arms and heaved for breath. Her ass rose to grind with his hips and she could feel his cock circling inside her, swaying and plunging, teasing and torturing. Her nerve endings began to sing in exquisite awareness. The hard rim ringing his head rolled up and down her length, stroking her ultra-sensitive walls and awakening the pleasure sensors in her entire body.

Endorphins popped around in her brain, bouncing off the fortifications guarding her emotional centers and setting up a vague sense of alarm that rocketed toward logic and reason like scud missiles.

"Scream for me, Kira. Scream my name when you come."

"Jack," she loudly complied.

"I love fucking you."

Shock shut her up. She'd never engaged in dirty bedroom talk. Never even imagined doing so. But if the sudden throbbing in her pussy was anything to go by, she supposed dirty talk had its uses. "Then fuck me. Fuck me, Jack." The words, hanging between them, clinging to her tongue and making her want to wipe them off in his mouth, incited a riot.

While the great sea-creatures rocked amongst the waves, he rocked into her with increasing force, gripping her hips and whetting his cock in her cunt 'til the heat and friction inside her threw off sparks.

With desire glazed eyes, and a passion drugged mind, she watched his reflection in the window as he used one hand and his teeth to rip his shirt over his head and onto the floor. Then he bent low over her back. She felt the prickle of chest hair against her spine and one hand coiling down her leg while the other reached for a nipple and pinched hard. Electricity jolted her, made her wetter, and incited a burning urge to bite him.

Her own reaction to his animal lust felt profoundly primal and wild and unlike anything she'd ever experienced in her life. Something else was going on here besides sex. He was coming for her with a power akin to unleashed madness and her arms were opening in welcome.

In surrender.

Whoa! Back up a second here. This had not been on her shopping list for the day.

He kept her movements under tight rein, controlling them with the vigor he'd displayed at the jet controls in rough weather, fine tuning a turn of hip, bracing her with subtle motions in his leg, like a foot on a rudder pedal. It struck her that he was flying her body, making it submit to his commands. She'd never been possessed so thoroughly. His cock battered at her protective barriers and she felt them giving with each thrust. She began to get hypnotized by the quick violent rhythm. Part of her felt it would be so easy to draw back the locks and let him come in. But if she did, entrapment of her heart would follow. It seemed like that indeed was his target area, that her heart was what he truly aimed for and was using his cock to spear it.

But why? He didn't want it. More than that, *she* didn't want him to have it. Not yet. Not this early in the game. Neither of them was ready for such an emotional cataclysm. And even if she had been, he wouldn't appreciate the easy victory. Men seldom did.

Hold back girl, you'll regret it if you don't.

She tried to re-focus on the purely physical sensations. There went his hands fisting in her hair, drawing her head back like a rider reining a horse. His hot spurts of breath fanned her shoulder blades and the air became so saturated with his need to control she could taste it.

The muscles in her pussy began to contract. Jack groaned and thrashed into her. Relentless. Consuming. Pounding so hard she feared he would reach her throat and his cum would spill out of her mouth.

"Stop," she yelled. He hesitated for a microsecond then picked up the pace again. Desperate for some emotional leverage and control of her own, she reached back and shoved him off her, standing up straight and whirling to face him.

"Kira?" His eyes held a pained expression. "Don't do this to me."

Her gaze locked with his and the dam inside her broke. "I'll do anything I want." Then she grabbed him by the shoulders and started nibbling on his neck. His thick skin, salty with sea mist and sweat, bunched succulently into bite-sized pieces between her teeth. She gobbled up and down the firm ridge of his shoulder and ran her tongue fully across his fuzzy pecs before damply tracing his collarbone and flicking the tip into the hollow at his throat. He shuddered in surprise, arms hanging limply at first but then snaking around her waist and gluing her against his torso.

She found tender slips of skin near his armpit and bore down sharply with her incisors. He flinched. His fingertips dug deeply into the flesh of her waist, punishing her for the assault and setting up a pleasure-pain reaction in the deep wells of her being. She burrowed her mouth into his chest and snagged a nipple.

"I hate this," he yelped with a shiver. "God. Don't stop."

The need to hurt him swelled up in a mesmerizing wave. Not hurt him a lot. Just a little. An urge to protect herself, she supposed. She'd never thought of sex as an attack and defend tool until now and was surprised at the raw erotic power of such a weapon.

Would this one, isolated event coming so early in their relationship cause a permanent erosion into sexual warfare? No way did she want that to happen.

While she hovered on the verge of softening and pulling back Jack picked her up, flipped her over onto the carpet and pumped into her from the front and she forgot everything but her body screaming for release. The thundering of the whales outside masked her cries. She clung to him as he bucked madly inside her, straining for his own release until he found it and slumped damp and replete over her wondering, quivering form.

He was not going to conquer her heart, body and mind. Not this time in this angry way. For now she'd have to gird herself until she felt safe. If that day ever came.

* * * * *

"Want to talk about it?" Kira asked later as they lounged on the sofa and fed each other fresh fruit salad from the buffet. The sun-warmed, overstuffed leather cushions enveloped her in cozy, lazy luxury and the companionable silence she and Jack had fallen into for the last few minutes encouraged her to probe for some answers.

"About what?" Jack asked, idly scratching her leg, which lay across his lap.

"About what just happened between us. It felt angry."

He snorted out a laugh. "Felt good to me. About time we went at it like monkeys." He popped a few chunks of ripe cantaloupe into his mouth and wiped his chin. "Later, I want to soak you in fruit juice and lick it off."

Sounded good to her. "Be serious for a minute."

He glanced at her. "Why?"

Was he being deliberately obtuse or was he genuinely confused? Either way would mean a wrestling match to get her answers. Did she truly want to go into the ring? Maybe certain things were best left unsaid, unexplained…unresolved. Then again, maybe not.

"Because I got the feeling we weren't really having sex. I thought it felt more like a power struggle." But over what? she silently questioned, and retraced the last hour to find out what set him off.

"Struggle over who would get the other off first, maybe," he said. But he tensed up and ran a rough hand over her thigh. "Honey, you got to stop thinking. Rule number one."

Typical Jack response. She decided to dig deeper with the germ of an idea. "Do you ever get upset about your mother? About when you left home?"

"I didn't leave," he said. "And to answer your original question, no. I don't want to talk about it."

Kira dipped a strawberry into a fondue pot of melted chocolate and teased his lips with it. The action caused him to drop guard long enough for her to slip in her trump card. "I never thought it bothered you, until you said that about the male whales." And that had indeed been the kicker. His entire personality had changed on the spot.

Jack bit the berry a little harder than necessary then looked at her like she was crazy. "Male whales get kicked out. It's a fact. Doesn't bother me."

"It *is* a natural fact. Just sounded like you took it personally." She'd endured enough upheaval at her father's death to know the value of a short visit in denial. But it looked like Jack had taken up permanent residence. It couldn't be good for him, to have ignored the pain of parental abandonment for so long. She wondered briefly if her parents had ever gotten counseling for him, but rejected the notion almost immediately. Her father believed in maintaining a stiff upper lip, and her mother would've most likely let him decide what to do.

"You heard wrong."

She'd been too young and self-absorbed to give his anguish a second thought. If she'd thought of it at all, it would've been to acknowledge how lucky he'd been to have her parents to fall back on. Now, though, she bet he hadn't felt lucky at all and a surge of belated guilt flooded her. At times like this, she really missed Mike and his other-worldly spiritual awareness. He'd know what to say whereas she would just have to wing it. "Do you ever miss her?"

"No." His voice cracked. "She went her way and I went mine. "

She tried to imagine what that would feel like and her heart shut down for a beat. "It must have hurt you, though. I know if it'd happened to me–"

"Kira. " He sighed. "It happened a long time ago. I moved on. End of pity party."

Yeah. Right. Sure. "Okay," she shrugged. "Have it your way."

Jack pushed her leg off with ill-contained impatience and got up to put on his jeans. "Don't start analyzing me."

"I was just wondering—"

"Don't. It's not worth it."

"Jack, for crying out loud. We're friends. You're worth it."

He turned and smiled at her, but instead of feeling warmed and reassured, Kira got a chill. "I didn't say I wasn't worth it. What's past is past."

Liar. Her unease kicked up a notch. She'd never seen his eyes so dead and soulless, and she began speculating whether they'd made a mistake by upsetting the status quo. Did his dark mood and the way he'd just made love to her have more to do with anger over his mother and this conversation, or with Kira herself? He'd seemed fine before they became lovers. Maybe he was worried she'd renege on the layover deal and ask for more.

Her heart took a nosedive. That was it. She knew it as certainly as she knew Jack. Tomorrow they'd be flying home and he was stressing. The fact that he didn't want her intruding on his psyche was proof enough. Lovers intruded. But there would be none of that between them, because they weren't real lovers. The line had been drawn.

Why did it cause an agonized pang? She'd known from the beginning Jack had limits. Hell, she'd known her whole life. Hadn't stopped her though. Why should the addition of sex make her feel wounded about it now? Stupid, stupid, stupid.

"Fine." She forced brightness into her voice. "No psychobabble, just sex on the run and the usual at home."

He had his back to her, gazing out the window. Kira could've sworn his shoulders slumped at her words. Out of relief, she thought.

"That was the agreement," he said, turning his head slightly, not looking at her.

"No need to remind me. I was the instigator."

Jack nodded and returned his scrutiny to the sea. Kira sat alone on the sofa and reminded herself that this was what she'd asked for.

* * * * *

Nice reality check, Grayson, Jack thought, your buddy Kira agreeing it's natural for women to discard men. Well, it was. Jack knew that better than anyone. Downright decent of Kira to give advance warning. One of her many admirable traits.

So why did he feel so lousy?

He watched the whales circling, pondering the fate of the young, innocent males who seemed so happy and carefree now. You just wait, he thought.

He should be high as a kite after a day of Kira. She was the best he ever had. More than the best. Sex with her flung him to heaven on a slingshot. He could come simply by looking into her eyes.

Perhaps that was the problem. It was too good. Felt too right. Better not get used to it. Home was only a heartbeat away. He'd go his way and she'd go hers.

Yippee. Couldn't wait.

Jack rolled his head. When was their next flight? Oh yeah, next week to Fairbanks. Long layover there while another crew took the plane to Tokyo and back. That would be fun. The sun would shine all night—no chance of sleep. Jack smiled, feeling better already.

In fact, he felt good enough to take a break from her when they got to New York. Yeah. That was the ticket. Just what he needed. Maybe he wouldn't call for a day or two, underscore the deal and give her a chance to hook up with someone else. He could work it that way. Not a problem.

His stomach sank.

Strange. He must be hungry.

Plans firmly in place, grin firmly on face, he turned and said, "Let's buzz the servants and order lunch."

Chapter Six

Moral dilemma number six –
Is all really fair in love and war?

The next morning in her hotel room, Jack hung up the phone, his mouth a tight line. "Well what do you know. A category two hurricane is piggybacking the tropical storm up the coast. They're expecting record storm surges along western Long Island. If the system takes the expected path, we'll get home by the skin of our teeth. Gonna be hairy going in."

"If it gets there sooner, they'll close JFK." The possibility of a few more days with Jack wound around Kira in a curling ribbon of delight.

Jack rose from the bed and zipped into his uniform trousers. "Now wouldn't that be a nightmare."

His wolfish grin heated her up. Their day and night together had evaporated too quickly. After that brief, awkward moment when she'd attempted "analyzing" him, they'd enjoyed a languid afternoon of lovemaking while the boat returned to Everett, followed by a night in and out of the tub.

The strength and endurance of their passion seemed boundless, like two people who'd never had sex before. She'd begun to believe she hadn't. Not really and certainly not like this. Whatever it was that she'd had with other men seemed feeble. Inept. Virginal.

Jack certainly knew his way around a woman's body. She refused to think about how and when he'd learned. And with whom. Preferring instead to be in the moment and accept his repeated assertion that he'd never had it this good.

In the throes of ejaculation he seemed to forget himself and become less conscious of his careful words. But she declined to take even that too seriously. It was easy to offer up mushy declarations when there was no blood in your brain.

Now it was time to face the music.

"Usually, I'm anxious to get home," Kira ventured. And it was true. She liked sleeping in her own bed, eating her own food, waking up to sun in the windows.

That's why she'd stuck to milk runs at Seaboard Express for so long. When she'd first considered flying for Pan Air, the idea of being away a night or two bothered her. At heart, she was a homebody, preferring the slapping surf of the beach to the honking and cursing of New York City, or any other city for that matter.

Jack, on the other hand, seemed to feed off city energy. The view from his pad was breathtaking—encompassing most of the Upper East Side—but Kira drew her energy from nature, strolling the boardwalk at night, watching the children in her community play.

Atlantic Beach lay under the approach path to the airport, and a hop skip to Manhattan, but the intrusion of landing jets was the only reminder of the nearby congestion. Somehow, it had maintained the lazy flavor of a beachside community even as property values had skyrocketed. In Atlantic Beach she could reach her mother's house within a few hours, and Jack or Lea within a few minutes. Kira was there to stay.

As long as her condo didn't get washed away.

"Not anxious to get home now?" Jack came over to pull her against him. "Not sick of me yet?"

"As if." She nuzzled his throat, inhaling him, absorbing this moment to savor later, when she was alone again with only the next layover to look forward to. "You're not sick of me, already, are you?"

"Not particularly."

"When's our next trip?" She certainly knew. She wanted to see if he was thinking about it too, looking forward to it as much as she.

He tweaked her nose. "Counting the days? Bad sign, hon."

Kira tried to ignore the veneer of dread around her heart. They dripped sarcasm on each other all the time, why should now be any different? She didn't want Jack to change completely just because they'd made love. Still, a romantic word or two out of bed might be nice.

As usual, he looked magnificent in his uniform. Now she knew how he looked underneath, what he moved like, felt like. She sighed. Only one thing between them had changed. He was still Jack, and he didn't want a steady relationship. She had to deal with that. Somehow, though, it seemed to be getting more difficult to do so. Uncertainty about her future with him and whether their friendship would survive the back-and-forth between lover and platonic lodged uncomfortably in her psyche. The stress made her heart pound at odd moments, similar to what might've happened in high school when she caught an unexpected glimpse of her crush *du jour* in the hallways.

It was just the sort of upsetting, nonstop head rush she hated living with on a constant basis. It messed with her mental health. Had she really blown it big-time by sleeping with him? Only time would tell.

They got to SeaTac with two hours to spare and Jack immediately logged into the computer for the latest weather. While the rest of the crew milled around with coffee, Kira listened to his report.

"It's been upgraded to a category three. Name's Liberty." Jack snorted, glancing over his shoulder. "Bearing down on Atlantic Beach within twelve hours, babe. You're not going home."

"Isn't that premature?" Kira shook her head. What a worrywart. "It might die before then, or go south."

"Maybe." He got up and stretched. Kira handed him a cup of coffee. "I hate you on the first floor."

"Don't even start."

"When you went to buy that place—"

"You're such a broken record. Chill. I'll be fine."

"And now, with Mike in Colorado, you have no place to bunk."

"There's Lea." Whoa, was she going to be flattened by Kira's news. For years she'd been trying to convince Kira of the benefits of casual sex. While not exactly a slut, she knew how to have a good time. Lea seized opportunities Kira didn't even realize existed and boldly dated men she didn't particularly like, just to leave all doors open and see what might happen.

While Kira had always been able to do that with travel opportunities, the layover deal was such a marked departure from normal operations Lea was going to be stunned.

"She's next door in Long Beach!" Jack howled.

"What about Mom out in Montauk?"

"You're not getting anywhere near there in this weather."

"Your place?" The pained look on his face cracked her heart. "Forget it." What had she expected? That he'd suddenly welcome a lover into his everyday life with open arms? This was idiotic. Kira mentally throttled herself. She had to stop thinking this way, expecting things. It wasn't part of the deal she herself had proposed. And she didn't want more than Jack was capable of giving anyway. Did she?

"You can stay with me if you have to," he said levelly. "I just hope it doesn't come to that."

Kira was beginning to hope so too.

* * * * *

Hours later they circled JFK in the teeth of a gale. Jack smiled grimly and armed the speed brakes. "Crosswinds at forty knots," he said. "Wind shear reported."

They received clearance to wrestle the monster to ground.

"Surf City here we come," Kira said.

Wind and rain slapped ferociously against the fuselage as they descended. Visibility hit zero. Kira glued her gaze to the instruments, secure in Jack's expertise and intuitive skill. He'd flown in incredibly hazardous conditions—landing on pitching navy vessels, in the rain, in the dark. The only difference here was the size of the machine and the three-hundred-some-odd passengers white-knuckling the armrests. And, oh yeah, level ground.

Easy as pie.

Jack brought them down as smoothly as he could, but a sudden gust ripped underneath at the last minute and bounced them up again. The plane thudded to earth a blink later and Jack retracted the reversers and headed for the gate.

"Nice," Kira said. "More like that and I'll need a mouth guard."

"Should've let you handle it, hot shot."

She laughed.

"Hey. Did you hear that? We have the distinction of being the last plane in," Jack said.

"They closed the airport?"

"Yup. Just now. Everyone else gets an expenses-paid trip to Philadelphia."

Unbelievable. "Not sure that makes me feel a whole lot better," Kira said.

"It's my first time closing the airport," Jack said proudly. "I should get a plaque."

"Better than a headstone."

Jack made the announcement to a weak flurry of applause, and Kira stood at the door to thank the pale-faced passengers as they hurried into the airport. While her attention was diverted helping a young mother and child, Svetlana squeezed past into the cockpit.

"That was marvelous, Jack," she cooed.

"Didn't do it alone," he said.

"But you did it just the same. Where'd you disappear to in Seattle, anyway? I wanted to get together but you were never in your room."

"People to see, places to go. What happened to Arlo?"

"Oh. He's…nothing. How about seeing me, going somewhere with me?"

There was a long silence. Kira strained her ears.

"Sounds good, Svet."

A burning began behind her eyes. She couldn't listen anymore. Somehow, she'd denied the reality of what coming home meant. The passion they'd shared, the laughter, meant nothing to Jack. Her body was the same as any other body. He'd had his fill of that new car smell.

She wondered when she'd get her two weeks' notice. He'd promised not to sleep with anyone else while with her, and Kira knew he meant it. Jack was nothing if not honorable. At least to her.

Before any tears spilled, Kira dove for the lavatory. She blotted her eyes, took a deep breath and refused to feel anything more. Drawing on her military training, she pulled her cap down low, straightened her lapels and went back to the flight deck.

So what if he felt casual about her? She felt the same way about him. She just slipped for a few hours. Thirty-six, to be exact. But that wouldn't happen again. From this moment she would have no further expectations. She was going to enjoy Jack while he lasted. But that didn't mean she couldn't try to make him last as long as possible.

Svetlana had slithered to the galley where she was talking animatedly with another attendant.

"Where'd you go?" Jack looked up from the parking checklist.

"I had to pee, do you mind?"

"Glad you didn't leak during landing."

"It was a close call."

"That was an anus-clencher all right. I plucked two buttons off my seat." Jack made a show of looking underneath his butt.

"You're a pig, you know that?"

"It's in my job description."

"Then how come *I* don't oink?"

Jack stared at her, a faraway expression in his eyes. "You might not oink, but you sure can squeal," he said at last.

The recollection set up a juicy throb between her legs. Jack could make her squeal all right, louder and longer than anyone else ever managed. *Time to put those memories into the box*. She cleared her throat. "We better get a move on if we're going to get home."

Jack snapped out of his trance. "I don't want you in Atlantic Beach for this storm."

She held up a hand. "Save it. The latest news from the control tower didn't mention any evacuations."

"We'll see."

"No *we* won't see. I can't stay with you."

"Why not?" Jack unfolded from the seat to gather his gear.

Kira blocked his path. "A—you don't want me there. B—we have a deal." *And C—it'd be torture for me to be near you without touching you.*

Jack tipped his head back and rolled his neck. He'd been doing an awful lot of that lately. "This is an emergency, Kira. It doesn't count."

She drew herself up, making full use of her height, but she still felt puny next to Jack. "What if I don't want to be there?"

His eyes flashed. "You don't have a choice. Look," he pushed his cap back and scrubbed his face. "It'll only be for two nights, tops. I know you love your beach, but face it, sweetheart, it might get washed away and I don't want you going with it."

She needed her bed, dammit. She needed the comforts of her own home to think about Jack and what her next plan of action would be. He was only doing this out of a misguided sense of responsibility. He didn't really want her there. "What about our deal?"

Jack's eyebrows shot up. "What about it?"

"You don't think it's going to be difficult to stick to it if we stay together two more nights?"

He shrugged. "Not for me."

Crap. She wanted to kick the shit out of him. "Fine!" Turn it off at will, make her feel like a flop in the bedroom. That was her Jack. Yes, sir. How much more of his insulting behavior could she take?

She snuck a glance at him through slitted eyes. He looked so complacent, so sure of himself. Well, Kira would see how strong he actually was. Her heart lifted and the clouds cleared. Cap'n Jack was about to meet his match. She'd make sure there was absolutely no touching, but boy was she going to tempt him. Torture him, to be precise. She felt an evil smile curve her lips. He said it would pose no problem to play hands-off.

Let him prove it.

*****

This was bad. Jack willed his hands to stop shaking as he gathered his stuff and prepared to leave the plane.

She didn't want to come home with him.

Fine.

She wanted to make sure he remembered the damn deal.

Fine.

But there was no way in hell he was letting her go back to her condo. He had to regroup. Get into a different head. Back to friendship mode.

He could stop looking at her, thinking about her, hearing her moans in his dreams. He'd have her next week again. Only seven short days. He could bear that. Yes, he could. And she would only be in his condo for two of those days. Completely manageable.

If he cut off his dick.

There had to be another way. Maybe he could wrap it in a bandage and cut off circulation. Maybe he could simply stay drunk. But he'd have to quit drinking two days before the next flight to clear his system.

Think, Grayson. Think!

There had to be a pill for this. They had a pill for everything these days. Too bad drugs would get him fired too.

Well, he had willpower. He did. He'd learned that in the Navy. What was that lesson? Jack couldn't recall. Maybe he'd been absent that day. Great.

He had no defenses left, except pretense. He could do that in spades—like before, when he'd shrugged and said *not for me*. She'd bought it easily enough. He could tell by her peeved expression.

And she'd been peeved all right. Jack knew that face. Had seen it all his life. Well, she couldn't have it both ways. She kept throwing the deal in his face and then getting pissed off when he stuck to it. Women.

"Find out where Lea's going," he ordered. If push came to shove, he could wrangle Lea into staying with them. That would certainly cool his jets. Although he didn't hate Lea, she ticked him off big-time. Especially the way she encouraged Kira to date losers.

Lea liked a trophy man on her arm and didn't seem to care if the trophy had a huge anus for a head. The men she fixed Kira up with made Jack see white.

They clunked up the jetway to the concourse and Kira pulled out her cell phone. Jack noticed Lea held the coveted number one spot on her speed dial. What was he, star sixty-nine?

They clicked along, the rolling luggage and chatter of people making it impossible to hear what Kira said. Finally, she folded the phone and dropped it back in her purse.

"She's in Riverhead with her folks. They evacuated the western barrier beaches."

"See? I was right."

"You were right."

What good was being right when you had the Empire State Building wedged in your pants and a woman who had a "deal"?

By the time they hopped the crew bus to the employee parking lot, Jack had a headache as huge as his hard-on. There wasn't one centimeter of him that didn't hurt. And it was all Kira's fault.

She settled next to him and he caught a whiff of damp sex. The drive into the city was going to be hell-on-wheels. Made worse by the smell of wet Kira in the passenger seat.

Wet Kira.

Jack shivered. It made him crazy, how ready she was. Anytime, anywhere. And it had provided his biggest surprise about her yet. All he had to do was look at her and she oozed. Was she this way with everyone?

Don't go there.

He sat back and tipped his cap over his eyes, savoring the echoes of her flavor in his mouth. If he concentrated, he could still taste her, smell her, feel her warm, tight wetness surround and engulf him.

Amazing how the slide of her stomach across his felt so safe, so comforting, even while they were going at it like monkeys.

Too bad he was only imagining such security. No way could it be anything but a fantasy. Women were good at that, lulling a man into a false sense of well-being, pretending love could cure anything.

The bus ground to a halt at the entrance to the employee parking lot. In deference to the weather, the driver took directions and inched through the lot, letting crew off at their car doors. Jack's ice-blue BMW shone like a wet jewel amongst all the black SUVs and white minivans. He loved that car.

Braving the lashing rain, he hopped out of the bus, unlocked the passenger door for Kira then ducked back inside for the luggage.

"Shouldn't we stay at the airport hotel?" Kira asked, once they were safely tucked inside.

"I'm going for it," he said. "Once we get over the bridge, it'll be nothing."

The drenching rain had rid him of his painful erection. No way was he going to destabilize again by checking into a hotel with Kira.

"We can get separate rooms."

Between the snakes in his stomach, and steel trap around his neck, Jack felt like he was falling apart. True, he wasn't getting any younger, but at thirty you wouldn't think a man would have these problems. "Chill. We're going home."

* * * * *

Kira saw the determination on his face and sighed. If it took all evening, he'd get them back. He was the safest driver in the galaxy. No fears about that. She was just bucking for more sex.

Overnight, she'd become a sex maniac. In one short day Jack had turned her into a simmering pot of lust. The thought of going without him for a week was driving her bonkers, and she'd just been laid "but good" not twelve hours ago. "There's the Pan Air Guest Lodge," she said as they whizzed past. "Wasn't that an Airport Inn?"

"Save it."

Now that she'd truly decided to pursue him for nothing but pleasure, to expect nothing from him but blasting orgasms, freedom spread through her with the freshness of a peppermint condom.

A little friendly persuasion was in order. "I want to make an addendum to the deal."

"What?" His voice squeaked. Puddles splashed. Thank God the roads were empty because he swerved slightly. "You just made an addendum. Only one addendum allowed."

"That wasn't in the deal."

"Neither were the addendums."

"I want more."

His knuckles went white on the steering wheel. "More what?" he asked through his teeth.

She let him suffer a minute. "I want more sex."

The relieved breath spewing from his chest blended with the howling wind outside. "Just more sex?"

"Lots of sex."

"What we had in Seattle wasn't enough?" His voice got squeakier.

"Oh that was dandy. Honestly. I meant tonight."

"Only tonight?"

"And tomorrow night."

Halogen headlights raced toward them, highlighting Jack's face into a lavender glow of terror. He didn't respond.

"I want sex all the time."

"Can we discuss this when I'm not driving in a hurricane?"

They could, but then she'd lose the upper hand. "You spoiled me and now you have to fix me."

"I can't fix you," he grunted. "You're hopeless."

"Rewind. Having sex with you spoiled me. Only more sex will fix me."

He looked like a boy who'd lost a puppy. "I guess I should feel good about that but sorry. No can do."

She wasn't going to take no for an answer. "I'm not asking for much. And really. Why shouldn't we extend the layover deal to include real life?"

"I liked the first deal."

"So did I but it's not enough."

A moment of thought. "How do you know? We only tried it once."

More than once, but she wasn't going to quibble. "Once wasn't enough. I don't want to go a full week without sex. I've gone without sex too long in my life as it is."

"A week isn't that long."

"It is to me."

Heavy sigh. He turned on the radio. "I knew this was a bad idea."

She turned it off. "It's not a bad idea. It's a great idea. You just have to get used to it." *Or have it pounded into your thick-ass skull.* What was wrong with him? According to Lea most men would leap at such an offer. Was it her? Was she not good enough? *Don't go there.* She was plenty good. Jack told her so and he didn't have a dishonest bone in his body. Unless you counted bon*ers*. She snickered to herself.

"Don't get me wrong, Kira. I love having sex with you. But I told you up front that I don't want a relationship."

"I'm not asking for a relationship." She flipped down the visor and checked her teeth in the mirror, trying to appear casual but starting to shake inside. Why was it so easy for most women to get casual sex, but so damn hard for her? Was she being punished in this life for promiscuity in a past life? Come on! "I'm asking for sex."

Jack didn't buy it. "This is how it all starts." He spread his fingers like little wings along the steering wheel.

"Someone changes the rules one by one until bam. You're married."

"You don't have to worry about that."

"Why not?" he asked quickly.

She narrowed her eyes at him. "Because I'll never marry a man who doesn't want to be married."

He chewed on that while they tooled up FDR Drive dodging potholes and puddles. True to Jack's forecast, the weather had calmed somewhat after they'd gotten away from Long Island's south shore, but rain was still falling in fat tropical sploshes. When they pulled into his underground parking garage, he said, "No."

They argued for forty floors in the elevator. Jack let them into his posh pad and she was momentarily distracted from her mission by the view.

Spectacular. Every time she saw it, she felt awed by the majesty of the soaring skyscrapers, the lights, the magical pulsing energy. While she would rather be standing on the beach at this moment, enjoying the fury of the coming storm, she had to admit that hovering high above it all in an aerie had its moments too.

Poised at the window, she saw Jack in reflection. He peeled off his jacket, loosened his tie and rolled his head.

"We're sticking to the original deal, plus the no-recycling addendum and that's it."

"Why?" she whined, her back still turned.

His arms pinwheeled helplessly and she smiled to herself.

"You'll never snag a husband if you're boogying with me all the time. That's why."

"Who said I wanted a husband?"

He plopped down in his nappy green sectional. "Don't be stupid. You were made for hearth and home."

Probably true. But she wanted adventure first. And she wanted it with Jack. He wanted it too. Why he was resisting so rabidly was beyond her. She'd get the scoop soon enough. Smirking at her reflection, she played her trump card. "Fine. I'll call Arlo."

For a guy who just wrestled massive tonnage in a windstorm, he moved pretty quick. Before she could blink he stood behind her, hands hovering in the air above her shoulders. "You have to give two weeks' notice."

"No I don't."

He howled. "You're reneging. You still have to give me next week and the week after. And after that…" he trailed off.

"After that, what?"

Jack's hands pumped into fists. "You're not calling Arlo."

True. She wasn't. But he didn't need to know that. "It'll be none of your business who I choose to have sex with."

"You'll always be my business."

"Not when the two weeks are up."

"Then you agree to the two weeks?"

She shrugged limply.

"This isn't fair. I need a drink." He stalked off to the kitchenette and, losing sight of him in the window, Kira focused on her own reflection. The twinkling lights of the skyline outside paled in comparison to the light of triumph she glimpsed in her eyes.

Chapter Seven

Moral dilemma number seven –
What's a little sexual harassment among friends?

Jack returned with two cold beers and forced one into her hand. "Drink this. Maybe it'll knock some sense into you."

He strode into his bedroom, emerging a few minutes later in gym shorts and a v-neck T-shirt.

Once again his physical beauty smacked her upside the head. Broad shoulders and chest, lean waist and hips and those muscular legs that could literally drive her to paradise.

His dark, soft chest hair curled around the stretched-out neck of the T-shirt, which was so well washed, she could practically see through it. If it weren't for the sour puss, he'd be perfect.

He threw himself onto the sofa and began surfing channels on his plasma TV.

Too bad she only had the clothes in her suitcase to tempt him with tonight. Weather permitting, she'd make a lingerie run to some upscale Manhattan boutique tomorrow, but for now…

With a soft sigh she stripped off her jacket and began unbuttoning her blouse.

Sensing sex, Jack's frowning face snapped around. "What are you doing?"

"Getting comfy."

"Can you do it somewhere else?" He returned his attention to C-SPAN.

Kira unzipped her trousers and let them fall to the carpet. Jack took a hefty swig of beer and studiously ignored her.

"Man I can't wait to get out of this bra. Will you scratch my back for me?"

"Not on your life."

"Just a little? I'm itchy."

"Go away."

"I'll do yours."

"Kira," he clicked the TV off and threw the remote on the coffee table. "We're not having sex and that's final."

"Tell you what. We'll lick each other and call it square."

"Don't be ridiculous."

"Just a thought." Kira dug a big toe into the plush carpet and swung her leg on the axis it provided. At the same time, she reached behind and unhooked her bra, letting it plop to the floor. "Ah."

The central air conditioning had an immediate effect on her nipples so she spread her arms wide and caught Jack taking a peek out of the corner of his eye.

"Put that back on," he growled.

"I never wear a bra around the house."

"Then put this on." He stood up and yanked his T-shirt over his head, throwing it in her face and sitting back down. But not before she spotted the huge erection tenting his gym shorts.

Obediently, she slipped into the T-shirt, dropping her panties at the same time.

"Can't you take no for an answer?" His eyes shot flames and she had a twinge of conscience. How would she feel if he did this to her when she didn't want sex? But he did want sex. He just didn't know it.

"Not from you," she purred, straddling his bare thigh.

Her damp folds kissed his flesh as she slid up his leg, slanting her face close to his and fanning him with a whisper of breath.

"Kira, I mean it."

He looked so vulnerable sitting under her, bare-chested, exposed, his eyes dark and open—and full of misery.

Kira slouched, taking pity at last. If he didn't want her tonight, she'd make darn sure he felt differently in the morning. "Okay." She rolled off his lap and plopped onto the sofa.

He fell silent. The air grew heavy with suspicion. "That's it?" he finally asked, turning toward her.

"Yep."

"You're caving?"

She slid him a glance. "Don't you want me to?" He nodded doubtfully.

"Then I'm caving." She turned her face away, stuck out her chin and crossed her arms. If she didn't look at him, she *might* be able to resist tormenting him further. Was going to be hard though. She really, really wanted to get laid again.

Jack's lower lip rose to suck on the upper one. He folded his hands and twiddled his thumbs. "That was too easy. What're you up to?"

"Nothing," she said innocently.

"Don't scam me." He rolled his neck and she wanted to massage it, badly. Instead she braided her fingers and sat calmly beside him.

"Stop it," he said.

"Stop what?"

"I can hear you thinking so just stop it."

In the past Jack had accused her of driving him crazy. In actuality he needed no one other than himself to get him there. She pursed her lips to keep from smirking. "It's a free country."

"I know you're up to something." He bolted off the couch and paced in front of her, halting to stab a finger in her face.

Kira got up and petted his cheek. "You're imagining things. You must be exhausted. Go to bed and we'll discuss this in the morning."

"There's nothing to discuss."

"I'll take the sofa. Go to bed."

"Fine, but we're not discussing anything tomorrow."

"As you wish."

He crossed to his bedroom door and turned. "I'm not changing my mind."

She shot him with her index finger. "Gotcha."

"Don't get cute with me."

Cute wasn't what she was planning. "Quit stalling and go to bed."

"I'm not stalling," he howled. He took a step closer. "I'm emphasizing. Not stalling."

She took a step closer. "You're emphatic about not having sex. I understand."

"Why are you smiling?" He took two more steps.

"I can smile. It's allowed." She leaned in, brushing her breasts against his chest.

"Not in my house and not like that." But all the oomph had gone out of his voice. "You need to put those panties back on."

"Make me."

He grabbed her shoulders and pushed her onto the sofa, covering her with his big, muscular body. Kira's legs automatically wrapped around his waist as he took both her wrists in one large hand and pinned her arms over her head. "You listen to me—"

"You have my attention."

"This condo is my ship and I'm the captain."

"Aye, aye, sir. Request permission to come aboard."

Jack stared into her eyes, his breath spurting. Kira let her body sag underneath him, so they sank further into the soft pillows. After a minute, his body grew heavy as he, too, relaxed. She stared frankly back at him and his eyes softened, crinkling around the edges as his mouth curled into a grin.

"You're too much," he whispered, shaking his head. "You're just too much fun to be around."

"You're fun too," she said, heart hitching at the sincerity in his voice. Without knowing it, she'd been waiting for this moment and at the look in his eyes, her whole world shifted.

He gazed at her a while longer, while the yearning inside her grew, then he blinked and pushed himself up. "Put it in the vault until next week."

She scrubbed her face and huffed out a breath. Hot tears of frustration pricked her eyes. She'd been paid back. She deserved it. And it felt cruddy. Her whole body felt clogged, heavy, in need of a major blowout. "Jack—"

"Save it."

"Can't we negotiate?" He'd come this close to losing control, and now she was the one begging. Great.

"You can have the bedroom," he said.

"You need more space than I do."

"Kira, take the damn bed."

Without another word she picked up her uniform, grabbed her suitcase and took him up on the deal. Once she'd closed the door, she let the groan she'd suppressed exit full throttle.

How could he turn it off like that?

Jack was stronger than she was, she supposed, feeling a grudging respect for him. He stuck to his guns. He was a man of his word.

Unfortunately for her sex life.

She kicked her suitcase into a corner and flung herself on the bed, digging fingernails into her thighs as his scent wafted up from the pillow.

She'd learned a lot about her best friend this evening. He was made of sterner stuff than she'd imagined. They had a deal and despite his raging erection and his appreciation of her, he was going to tough it out.

And here she'd thought he was a lightweight. That he would crumple at the slightest sexual opportunity.

As she threw back his bedspread and snuggled between sheets that smelled of the elements, an admiration swelled in her heart that became as thick and as throbbing as the frustration between her legs.

Jack was a gentleman. In the truest sense of the word. In bed and out.

And that was good because?

She couldn't respect him if he wasn't. But even gentlemen had their limits. She could hear him slamming around the kitchen, unloading the dishwasher, banging the pots. Eventually, he moved to the linen closet and she heard the billow of heavy sheets as he shook them out.

Slowly but surely, he was coming unhinged. If she played it right, she'd have her gentleman friend in her bed all the time. And who knew what might happen after that?

*****

Nothing was going to happen. Nothing. Jack muttered, cursed, and spread sheets over the sectional. The king-sized seven-hundred-and-fifty-thread-count cotton felt thick and silky in his hands—like Kira's hair—but the sheets were too big for the sofa and he tripped over them twice trying to tuck everything in.

A metaphor for this relationship, he thought sourly.

He didn't want her to be fun, didn't want to want her, didn't want to need her. He had to remember that whenever those feelings erupted, which seemed to be happening a lot lately.

He wanted freedom from that kind of responsibility, that kind of *fear*. Because no matter how badly you wanted something, it could still disappear in a blink.

Like their deal.

In the span of thirty-six hours, she'd changed the rules twice. Jack felt betrayed. He'd trusted her! Kira had never broken a promise until now. Just went to show what happened once you had sex with a friend.

Big mistake.

He'd fooled himself into thinking it wouldn't backfire in his face.

Dumbass.

All women got possessive and demanding once they got laid. Why hadn't he remembered that before? He'd been a fool to make love to her. He was going to have to reconsider Plan A—marry her off. Even if it meant endorsing Arlo. Jack gritted his teeth.

No more layovers. No more sex. End of deal. Tomorrow he'd take her back to her condo and make her call The Scab.

Feeling better, he slid between the wrinkled mess of sheets and clicked on the TV news just in time to see Hurricane Liberty send the Atlantic Ocean ripping through Kira's condo. Update at six.

At his strangled yelp, Kira came rushing out.

"What's wrong?"

Jack scissored upright and clicked the TV off just as she got there. "Nothing," he squawked. "Everything's fine." *Except your home is under water.*

This was bad.

By now, dawn was breaking and a thin streak of purple sky lay outside his high-rise window.

Kira pushed a hand through rumpled hair and sat down beside him. "Why did you shout? It sounded like you saw an accident."

"Must have been having a nightmare." How in the hell was he going to break this to her? She loved that damn condo.

She eyed him quizzically. He tried to look innocent. She yawned and slumped. "I can't sleep anyway." A feline smile played around her lips. "Want to play strip poker?"

Jack's heart took an express elevator to his toes. "Kira, I lied. Something did happen."

She turned huge, round eyes on him and his throat clogged. He cleared it and said, "I'll make you breakfast."

"Who died?"

Shit. "No one. No one died, honey." He reached out and gripped the back of her neck and those beautiful green eyes filled up.

"Well, that's a relief."

"Come in the kitchen. You can make the coffee."

She padded behind him like a little girl and all his protective instincts roared to the surface. He remembered how she'd cocooned into him when her father died. How helpless he'd felt. And now all those memories were bubbling back, just when he thought it was over.

"It's got to be bad if you won't tell me. Was there a plane crash?"

"No. Nothing like that. Look." He raked a hand through his hair, needing time to figure out how to tell her. "Just wait for the coffee."

In silence she measured the scoops, filled the coffeepot and stood watching and waiting. Jack scrambled four eggs, made toast and by the time they carried the meal into the living room, bright sunshine streamed in.

Hard to believe a few hours ago a mighty storm had torn into everything Kira had left.

He closed his eyes and when he opened them she had her hands folded neatly in her lap and her lips pressed tightly. "You're breaking up with me, aren't you?"

Yes. No. What a mess. No way could he dump her now—hand her over to freaking Arlo.

She needed good news. Yeah. Good news. Something to deflect the horror she'd be facing. "I want an addendum to the deal." *No. No. No. Where did that come from?*

"You do?" She looked skeptical. Good. If she'd looked goopy he'd have hurled.

Jack tried to shake his head *no* but it somehow turned into a nod.

"You scared the crap out of me because you want an addendum to the deal?"

"Well, it scared me too." Understatement of his life.

Kira took a bite of egg. "Do tell."

With the brain cell he had left, he'd planned on simply jumping her bones and demanding sex twice a day until one of them died of it. But what came out instead was, "I think you should move in with me."

Her fork stalled in midair.

Jack took the ball and ran. "Might as well. We'd save money on house payments, transportation—"

"Jack—"

"Just think of the wear and tear on my car, driving out to Atlantic Beach to see you every day. That alone—"

"Jack!"

"Leave everything there. I'll buy you new clothes, new makeup. You won't even have to go back."

"I can't just stay here and never go back."

"Think of it as an adventure."

Her eyes narrowed and she pressed a palm to his forehead. "Have you been drinking?"

If only. "Sober as a deacon."

"You really want me to move in with you?"

Jack coughed. "Yes. Starting now. You go take a shower and I'll call an estate dealer to sell all your stuff. You can buy new stuff for here."

"I don't want to sell my stuff."

He looked at her like she'd gone mad. "Of course you want to sell your stuff. It's shitty, mismatched, old." *Soggy.*

"It took me ages to find all my treasures."

Yeah, he knew. She'd spent months decorating that dump, searching flea markets, antique shops, garage sales. And she'd done a damn fine job arranging the odd furniture and broken bric-a-brac. Even though it wasn't Jack's taste, he'd felt comfortable there. Now it was probably gone.

He remembered her saying she never wanted to own anything she didn't love. So she loved everything she owned. Dearly.

This was horrible.

"Tell you what. You list your favorite pieces, we'll have them cleaned and bring them here. The rest, you sell."

"Have them cleaned?"

Jack smacked his forehead. "Did I say *cleaned*? I meant cleared." She was looking at him strangely. "We'll have them cleared out. That's what I meant."

"I'm calling the doctor."

Oh hell. Jack shoved the dishes aside and tackled her.

Kira yelped as he hit full force and jammed her into the cushions. "You're crazy," she screeched. He started biting her neck.

"Crazy about you," he said through his teeth. He tangled her legs with his and locked her underneath.

*****

"I don't believe you." Something was wrong with this picture. Where had Gentleman Jack gone? Kira struggled half-heartedly, but he must've sprouted extra arms. He pinned her so efficiently she could barely move.

"What's not to believe? You're a gorgeous sex maniac. What man wouldn't want you living with him?"

"You, Jack."

He stopped kissing her.

"You don't want me here, so why don't you just tell me the truth?"

"I'd rather do this." He covered her mouth with his, tongue teasing her closed lips, hands roaming over her breasts.

Kira wanted answers and she wanted them fast.

Well, eventually, she did.

Her body started humming at his touch. Jack sensed her response and grew gentler, fingers slipping under her

T-shirt and circling her nipples as lazily as a hawk riding an updraft.

"You'd better not change your mind."

"No way," he said softly, stopping to gaze into her. Then his hips slid between her legs and she unwrapped to embrace him.

His lips wandered over her face in light, feathery kisses. Even his body on hers seemed lighter, slower, gentler than usual, as if his desperation had diminished and taken some of his intensity with it. Everything about the Jack making easy, sensuous love to her felt new and different and she couldn't put her finger on why, so she put her fingers on his ass instead. And pressed his erection hard into her crotch.

His head dipped down as he rolled her T-shirt up to her neck, exposing her breasts to an adoring visual inspection. "Did I mention how much I like these?" He braced himself on one arm and leaned back against the sofa cushions, fanning one large hand across her chest and breezing it over her flesh with reverential tenderness.

"You might have said something one or two hundred times," she smiled.

"Always considered myself an ass man until I saw these," he grinned. "Not that your ass leaves anything to be desired." He plunged his hand south and squeezed a cheek, making her giggle and scoot more securely beneath him.

"I like your chest." She reached out to stroke his fuzzy pecs, loving the soft, tickly sensation between her fingers but missing the feel of him against her own chest. Against her heart.

"My chest?" He sounded surprised and a confused frown line appeared over his nose. "And here I thought you were just in it for my cock."

"That too." They chuckled softly and he nuzzled her neck with succulent lips. Lowering his body in welcome contact against hers again, he ran a butterfly hand over her face and cleared stray hairs out of her eyes.

"I can't think of any part of you I don't like," he muttered and her heart hitched. She closed her eyes and savored the warmth of his breath on her face, the tingle of his chest hair and the beat of his heart. His body was a walking, talking aphrodisiac to her. She was beyond hope and he seemed relentless in his mission to keep her there.

His open lips sucked down her neck, across her chest and over each breast. Her fingers laced through his curls, holding him closer so she could feel the imprint of his face against her skin. His five o'clock stubble followed the trail of his tongue, feeling like the lick of a hungry lion and she arched into him as he slipped his shorts off.

"Condoms," she gasped. "In my suitcase."

Jack got up and carried her into the bedroom. "We needed to come in here anyway," he said, laying her on the bed and snagging a condom.

She unwrapped it and placed it over him, using both palms to unroll it in a caress.

"One of these days we'll have to christen other rooms," she said.

He lay down beside her and coaxed a hand between her legs. His middle finger caressed her slick opening in small, bobbing circles, slipping in and out tentatively, like the spy-hopping whales. He tormented her G-spot. Stroking with whisper-soft motions. Stopping. And stroking again. She began to pant for more, wanting to grab his hand and shove his fingers in deeper. Her hips rose and fell with mounting need.

"I like having you in bed," he murmured.

"Me too."

"Like this." He pulled her underneath him, separating her legs with his knees, and inched inside. "Call me unimaginative, but this is my favorite."

Kira gasped at the slow torture of his entry. This was her favorite too, having Jack's solid weight on top, feeling the way he chose to move inside her. And man did he know how to move.

His thrusts, lazy but powerful, felt like lapping tide against rocks. And like the tide, he seeped into every emotional crevice, refreshing her, bringing her back to life. Just as he'd always done—when he'd moved in with her family, after her father died and now, when he made love to her.

Through the shimmer of an approaching orgasm, Kira supposed she'd fallen in love with him, but the urgent needs of her body took precedence over the examination of her emotions. Jack's long, lazy strokes had quickened and shortened and they strained against each other until the explosion ripped through them, thrashing them around the bed in the kind of chaotic, pulsing climax that had become the hallmark of sex with Jack.

"See how good we are together?" he said through heavy puffs of breath, slumping over her in a damp tangle of limbs.

"I've only said that a million times," she said and scratched his back, sending him into groaning aftershocks.

"So you'll move in?"

Amazing he was still gnawing that bone. She'd kinda reckoned the orgasm would've relieved him of that particular, *insane* notion. "This from a man who wanted nothing but layovers a minute ago."

"Things change."

"Not that fast."

"I had an epiphany."

Kira pushed him away gently. He unlatched, sat up and fluffed a pillow behind her.

"C'mere," he said, pulling her into his arms. She snuggled into his furry warmth. "I want you here, with me."

This was nutty. Kira fingered his chest hair, spiraling it into a little garden of whorls. She couldn't quite buy into the sincerity in his tone, but she didn't want to blow him off completely. For whatever reason--he was obsessed with this idea of living together. Okay. She'd bite. "That's all well and good, Jack. But I don't like Manhattan."

"You love Manhattan."

"Not to live." Below on the street, a truck honked, as if to punctuate her statement. She wouldn't do well here on a permanent basis. Already she yearned for the desolation of the beach at dawn.

"What if you didn't have a choice?" Jack said softly.

The question, so unlike something Jack would ask, pressed a cold finger of fear against her heart. She remembered how he'd frantically switched the TV off when she charged into the room, the grave look on his face and how he'd deflected her worries with sex.

Come to think of it, that's how he'd always operated, with offers of treats like movies or ice cream when she felt low. He never could tolerate her being sad.

Suddenly, the suspicion that he'd sidetracked her by asking her to live with him rose like a sour burp in her throat.

"Is that a rhetorical question?" She almost gagged on the words and the expression he turned on her made her sick with fear. "You'd better tell me what's going on," she said. "I mean it Jack Grayson. What did you see on the TV earlier?"

He squeezed her tightly, pressing her head against his clamoring heart. "Atlantic Beach got massacred."

Chapter Eight

Moral dilemma number eight –
Deal Shmeal

"What?"

"Flooded out."

"That's what you saw on TV?"

Jack nodded grimly. "They showed the water hitting your condominium complex."

"Oh Lord." She went numb, blank. "Is it still there?"

"Yeah. But it's not going to be pretty."

"Are you sure it was my condo?"

Instead of arguing, like usual, Jack reached for the clicker and turned the bedroom TV on. Various clips of local thrill-seekers standing on the boardwalk and being lashed by wind and rain interspersed with later footage of buildings in her entire community getting torn asunder. Finally her precious home appeared. Then disappeared. During the endless minutes she watched in stunned silence, the horror replayed over and over, each time becoming more and more surreal until she finally made him turn it off.

Without warning, a searing fist of fresh worry lodged in her heart. "I'd better call Mom." She vaulted off the bed. Jack grabbed her before she got to the phone.

"She's fine. Montauk was spared, but she'll be worried about you. I should've called her but I didn't think of it."

He looked stricken, but it wasn't his fault. He'd been too concerned with taking care of her. She stroked his arm with clammy hands. "Don't worry about it."

"I don't know what's wrong with me."

"Nothing's wrong with you Jack. A lot has happened the last couple of days." Too much to bear thinking about. If she didn't kick her mind into autopilot soon she'd be heading in the general direction of the funny farm.

Kira dialed the number and her mother picked up before the first ring. "I'm fine Mom."

"Oh, thank God." Her mother's voice wobbled and Kira's eyes watered. "I was just going to call Jack. Where are you? I figured you didn't make it in last night after they closed the airport."

As Kira explained what had happened, self-induced numbness morphed into an urgency to be with her mother. Knowing Maggie, she'd have been up all night stressing. Something Kira could've alleviated if she hadn't become so sex-centered lately.

She felt disgusted with herself. "I'm coming out there, later," she finished. "But first I want to swing by my condo."

She became aware of Jack sitting beside her, rubbing her back, the lines around his mouth etched deeply in concentration. After a few more minutes of platitudes and I-love-yous from her mother, she hung up.

And dove into Jack's arms. He felt solid and safe, and the way he'd tried to make it better warmed her up and pissed her off at the same time. How dare he manipulate her emotions, use sex as a bandage. Yet how awesome of him to try.

He could be such a buffoon. He meant well, but he seemed clueless about how his method had messed with her head. She'd actually felt hopeful again. As if one day they'd have something more. Now she realized he was just being Jack The Protector. The role he played best.

"Thank God you weren't home," he murmured and she felt him tremble. "You would've drowned. Or been stranded on the top floor, waiting for one of those asshole ambulance-boats to float down the streets."

"They're not asshole boats. They save lives."

"Maybe." Jack snorted. "But you could've been there. I hate you there."

His tension was back. She could feel it in every fiber. She wondered why. He'd known about the disaster before they made love, yet he'd been so relaxed she'd barely recognized him. Now he was ready to blow.

"Whatever." He sat frozen for a moment then said, "Get dressed. Let's take a ride."

While she dressed in the cleanest clothes she had left, Jack tried calling the emergency centers. Failing to get through, he tried the Internet. Kira heard the telltale bling of an Instant Message.

"It's Lea," Jack said in a venomous tone. Kira took the seat he vacated, and heard him muttering as he left the room. Lea informed her the roads were closed and police were only allowing access to road workers and building inspectors for the time being. After an IM-free moment Kira sensed the burning question paramount in her friend's mind and her blood pressure soared. Sure enough, Lea asked whether there'd been any more *moments* with Jack.

Kira's fingers stalled on the keyboard. Were there moments? Yeah. Lots of moments. A shitload of moments and not all of them good. Though she yearned to give Lea a blow-by-blow and get her friend's advice on what to think and how to proceed, now wasn't the time to get involved in an analysis. Lea would demand uncensored details and provide extremely forthright and possibly rude recommendations. Kira could hear Jack rustling in the kitchen. He'd be poking his nose in any minute and if he caught sight of his name on the screen proceeded by *blowjob*, or *world-class jerk*, he'd freak.

Typing a quick goodbye, she signed off and scurried into his bedroom to reorganize her luggage.

After a while, Jack wandered in. "What are you doing?"

She tucked a strand of hair behind an ear and zipped the suitcase. "What does it look like I'm doing?"

Jack crossed over and took the suitcase. "You won't be needing this at your mother's." He opened the closet and shoved it inside.

Kira hauled it back out. "I'm staying with Mom."

"No you're not."

"I'm not going to argue with you. Mom's endured a lot of grief lately and she wants me there."

"Did she say so?"

"Not in so many words."

"Then you stay here."

Kira clenched her fists and counted silently to ten. She disliked being forced into anything, especially some twisted setup to soothe Jack's conscience. "I'd love to stay and play house with you Jack, but—"

"Is that what you think this is? Playing house?"

"That's exactly what I think it is. You had a knee-jerk reaction to the flooding—" *And right now my knee wants to jerk in the general vicinity of your balls* "—and made the mistake of asking me to live with you." Her teeth hurt. Her head hurt. Every single cell in her body ached in despair. Were *all* men such morons? Or was it just Jack's special gift?

"Maybe at first. But the idea grew on me."

Did he have a clue how stupid he sounded? Kira shook her head. "It was a lovely, spontaneous offer and I'll be grateful forever, but no thanks." The idea grew on him? Could he be telling the truth? She'd have to explore that later, after downing a fistful of pain relievers with a shot or two of heavy-duty liquor. For now she had ants in her pants for Montauk. Her brain had thickened and congealed with stress and she couldn't think beyond the trials of the next couple of days. If she started angsting about Jack she might lose it completely.

"If you stay there, it'll take you three hours to get to the airport every time we have a trip."

She hadn't thought of that. Blech.

"I'll come here the night before." At last, a trump card. She could see the frustration on his face as he tried to think up a comeback. "And if we get in late, I'll stay here until morning." Ha! "We can extend the layover deal to include those nights, since you don't really want sex to be part of our 'at home' relationship."

Was that cruel? It felt cruel. But a secret side of her did a happy dance. That would teach him not to use sex to manipulate her. Two could play that game.

He looked fittingly crushed. "I asked for an addendum."

"Addendum denied."

"I didn't deny yours."

"Yes you did. You denied my second addendum, which asked for sex twenty-four/seven. Then you commandeered it and pretended it was your addendum, to make me feel better about losing everything I have."

"Oh yeah." Jack raked fingers through his hair. His eyes narrowed. "Don't you still want sex twenty-four/seven?"

"Not if it's pity sex."

"Did this morning feel like pity sex?"

She had to sit down at the memory. No. It felt like lovemaking. In the truest sense.

Don't go there.

"There was a touch of pity."

"Nice try," he said softly.

She looked at him. He looked at her. Music blared. They both jumped. Jack strode to the nightstand and smacked his radio alarm clock. "Guess I had it preprogrammed for an appointment today. Doesn't matter now."

"It's eight o'clock already," she said, unwilling to explore the heaviness that had settled between them when she didn't know if she had a refuge anymore. "We need to get going. Traffic is going to be a nightmare."

Jack grunted a terse agreement. "We'll talk about this later." He strung her tiny purse over her shoulder and they began the arduous trek out to her mother's.

Following Tom Allen's death, her mother had retired full-time to the summerhouse they'd had for years. Normally, Kira enjoyed the scenic drive, but today vast quantities of humanity either returning home or venturing out from New York City to inspect vacation properties clogged every major artery through southwestern Long Island. Ever the optimist, Jack had decided they'd have better luck taking the central route. No dice. The Long Island Expressway lived up to its infamous reputation as the world's longest parking lot.

At her first glimpse of the congested ribbon, she'd tried to convince Jack to turn around. "Fuck the traffic. You need your mother," he'd stated firmly. Truer words had never been spoken. Aside from her father's death, Kira doubted there was ever an occasion when she needed her mommy more. Apprehension clawed at her shoulder muscles, shortening them and making her have to consciously stretch her neck every few minutes. What was she going to do? Where was she going to live? Would her condo have to be razed?

The uncertain turn life had taken was compounded by Jack. His motivations were questionable and she didn't feel strong enough to discuss living arrangements right now. So she didn't. Most of the ride was spent in silent worry.

By the time they hit Suffolk County, the traffic jam had essentially flip-flopped to the westbound side of the expressway and they managed to pull into her mother's driveway by early afternoon.

Her mother met them at the door. Jumping out of the car, Kira noticed her already-trim mother had dropped even more weight. She'd been steadily losing since Tom's death and it frightened Kira, reminding her of how thin her father had grown in his struggle against cancer.

"Two-thirds of my favorite people," Maggie said, trotting down the walkway and embracing them. "Mike called right after you did and I told him what happened. He wants you to arrange an emergency pass so he can come help."

"I'll take care of it," Jack said.

Kira's eyes welled up. So typical of Mike to drop everything when she needed him. And if anyone could wrangle a last-minute employee family freebie, it would be Jack. God. The men in her life rocked. Her parents had done an incredible job. "Sorry for worrying you, Mom," she said. "We got in late last night and I didn't know the storm hit so hard until this morning."

"I'm just glad you're all right."

"I should've called," Jack reiterated, slinging an arm around Maggie's thin shoulders and planting a kiss on her forehead. "How's my best girl?"

"Thankful that Kira has you to watch after her," Maggie said with a delicate shudder.

Jack met Kira's eyes over the top of her head. "Kira does well enough on her own."

Kira wrinkled her nose at his proud smile. "I certainly do, most of the time. But I was grateful for Jack landing that sucker yesterday."

"I didn't do anything you couldn't have done better."

"Except bring us down in one piece." The appreciation in his eyes warmed her to her toes. It was new for them to pay each other sincere compliments and even though she suspected it was only temporary—due to her situation—she still liked it. Mucho.

They beamed at each other a moment longer until Kira noticed her mother eyeing them. She quickly frowned and asked about lunch. Would not be cool if her mother found out about the layover deal.

They filed inside the kitchen. Maggie had set out a spread of deli sandwiches and salads. While they piled plates, Maggie dug out two cold beers and a bag of chips. "I'm sure you two have worked up quite the appetite," she said.

Sandwich wedged in mouth, Jack froze and fired a look at Kira. She grimaced and slanted a gaze to Maggie's beatific smile. Did she know?

Couldn't be. Probably just a guilty conscience on Kira's part. Kira shook her head at Jack and he resumed chewing.

It felt wonderful to be back in the kitchen of her childhood summers. The whole house was a time capsule of the Fifties. Especially the kitchen, with aqua metal cabinetry and stainless steel countertops. Shell pink tiles brightened the backsplash around the sink, and speckled pink and green linoleum completed the look.

Recently, Maggie had taken an interest in acquiring some of the original accoutrements that had gone missing over the years, and had somehow unearthed a white bullet-shaped refrigerator, among other things.

Once a shabby summer home, it had become a lovingly restored shrine to a man who had bought it for his wife on their tenth wedding anniversary.

Heart and stomach full, Kira rose to wander into the living room.

Maggie followed, saying, "Do you have a sense of how badly your condo was damaged?"

She sank onto the sleek, serpentine sectional. "Not really. It didn't look good on television, though."

Jack came in and sat next to her, slinging an arm across the low back and absently scratching her shoulder.

"Just remember, unlike people, things can be replaced," Maggie said. "See how easily?" She swept a hand around the living room. "I found that boomerang coffee table at a garage sale, day before yesterday. Your father used to love putting his feet up on one just like it. Drove me batty at the time."

"But I bet you'd buy him a zillion boomerang tables now," Kira said, swallowing a knot. In all this time, she hadn't thought once about her things. Not just *her* things, family things. Mementos.

"Yes. I would. But my point is that I replaced the table. You'll mourn for your things. But don't waste too much time on it because you can buy more."

"Not everything can be replaced," she whispered, remembering one item that held importance for them all.

"Things can be replaced. People can't," Maggie said firmly.

"Dad's cockpit briefcase is in my office," Kira choked.

Jack's hand fisted in her hair.

Maggie crossed her arms at the waist and brought a trembling finger to her lips.

"I should've used it. Then I'd have had it with me."

"It'll be fine," Jack said gruffly.

She turned to him and hiccoughed. "What if it isn't?"

No one said anything.

"I should've used it," she repeated. What was the point of keeping someone's material possessions around if they never got used? Someday she'd die too and leave her stuff *and* her dad's stuff behind. Shouldn't she enjoy it while she could? It suddenly seemed almost disrespectful not to.

Eventually, Jack ventured, "You didn't want the smell to go away."

She loved the way the inside of that old, musty Halliburton smelled. Truth? Jack savored it as well—the smell of early flight, glamour. Once in a while, she'd caught him sneaking a whiff. Now it might be lost.

"If it's still there, I'm using it," she said.

"I think you should."

"If it's still there." Her voice wobbled and she wiped her face with the back of her hand. "The antique wool Pan Air blanket was there too."

"It's up high, though. On the wall."

The next chilly night it'd be where it belonged. On her lap. "Dad's war medals."

"Mike has the Distinguished Flying Cross."

"And all my treasures."

Jack scooted closer, pulling her head onto his shoulder and stroking her face. His hand felt big and warm. His body, a haven. The new, intense physicality of their relationship seemed to pulse in the air and Kira sensed Maggie's antennae rise. She peeked out from under Jack's hand and caught a coy gleam in her mother's eyes.

Busted.

She'd get the Spanish Inquisition later.

"When can you take a look at the condo?" Maggie asked casually, brushing imaginary lint off crisp white shorts. Kira saw the wheels turning in her head.

"Tomorrow," Jack said. "Word on the radio is that the water's receding but they're not letting anyone in until they inspect the structures."

Leaning forward, Maggie asked, "Do you think Mike will make it out tonight?" The soft question galvanized Jack and he obediently got up to call Pan Air, leaving Kira alone with her.

"Slick, Mom. Real slick."

Maggie smiled. "When did all this come about?"

She could play dumb, but it seemed pointless. At twenty-eight she should be mature enough to discuss certain aspects of her sex life with her mother without being reduced to a quivering blob of anxiety. "Night before last. In Seattle," she stated matter-of-factly. But her hands started shaking.

"That recent?" Her mother sat back, thoughtfully scratching her arms.

"You don't sound surprised." And here Kira figured she'd go postal at the thought of her daughter sleeping around. Her mother's mild reaction shored her up and confused her at the same time.

"I'm only surprised it didn't happen sooner."

Huh?

"I mean it's about time. Goodness. Your father kept pestering me about it before he died."

"He did?"

Maggie sighed as if she'd reiterated this a thousand times. "He wanted to see you and Jack settled. I told him I had no control over your hormones."

Kira's jaw dropped. Her mother never talked like that. "What?" she stammered.

"Oh come on. Don't be naïve. It doesn't become you."

She snapped her mouth closed and straightened. "Dad wanted me and Jack to get married?" How come she was the last to know? "Did Dad talk to Jack about this?"

"I assume he did," Maggie said. "I know they had a long talk before he died and after that, Jack never left you alone. It took you an awfully long time to get the hint. And here I thought I raised a smart daughter."

So that was why he'd been behaving so strangely. Well, knock her over with a feather. "But he told me he doesn't want to get married."

"You believed him?" Maggie laughed out loud. "Darling, all men say that. Of course Jack wants to get married. To you."

"How can you tell?"

"You don't see how he looks at you when you're not looking, or his face when you leave the room, or his face when you enter a room. But I do."

"That's lust. Doesn't mean he wants to marry me." And boy had he been ultra-clear on that point. Her body started venting toxic fumes of anger at the mere memory. She was good enough to hang out with twenty-four/seven and have hot sex with, but to marry? Not a chance.

"What about how he takes care of you."

"That's some twisted sense of responsibility left over from when we were kids."

"Then why does he get between you and all your boyfriends?"

Why *did* he do that? Kira didn't know, but she said, "He thinks they're not good enough for me."

"He's measuring them by a yardstick called love. That's why."

"That doesn't make any sense—"

Jack ambled into the room. "Mike's on the last flight out of Denver. Arrives at midnight. I'll pick him up and he can stay with me and Kira."

"I told you I was staying with Mom tonight," she said, so wanting to continue the conversation he'd interrupted.

"Go with Jack, darling. I'll meet you in Atlantic Beach tomorrow."

Jack's triumphant look pissed Kira off so she dug in her heels. "I'll sleep here and we can drive out together," she said to her mother. "I'm sure Jack and Mike would enjoy a boys' night out on the town."

Jack dropped petulantly onto the sectional.

"Maybe you'll hook up with Svetlana," she added snidely. Now where did that come from? Oh yeah. From when she'd heard them cooing in the cockpit. Maggie was wrong. No way did he want to marry Kira with the blonde bombshell detonating on the flight deck.

"What's that supposed to mean?" Jack asked.

"Really, Kira," Maggie said.

"Never mind," she said miserably. "I'm sorry. Stress."

"I'll make you some iced tea," her mother said and left.

Jack didn't look mollified. In fact, he looked thunderous. Her and her big mouth.

"Walk me to the car," he ordered.

"You're leaving now?" She glanced at the clock and saw it was already pushing three. He'd get home at six and have to turn around and go to the airport after dinner.

What an awesome guy.

Suddenly, she felt guilty for making him go alone. But her only other option was to miss an insightful conversation with Maggie, forcing *her* to drive alone tomorrow. Life sucked sometimes.

Once outside, Jack sat her down on the hood of his precious car and loomed above. "Tell me what that crack about Svetlana meant."

She buffed the flawless finish of the car with her butt. Did she really want to start this, right before he left? She felt ridiculous. Underneath all the stress about her home, her worries and fears for her possessions and her future, jealousy was consuming her. She didn't have the right to feel jealous. She herself had proposed dating on the side. But she did feel jealous. In spades. "I heard what you said to her when we landed last night."

"Heard what?"

"When she asked to see you and you said yes."

Jack looked genuinely confused so she acted out the conversation, sparing Svetlana no mercy. When she finished he tipped his head back and roared.

"Glad someone thinks it's funny."

"Kira." He wrapped her in his arms and kissed her, hands roaming at will, lips moving lazily over hers. "You didn't stick around for the rest of the conversation," he said against her mouth. "When she asked if we could see each other and go places together I said, 'Sure. Anytime we bid the same flights.'"

Kira blinked. "You meant only when you work together, on the plane?"

"I was being sarcastic."

She sagged against him. "Bet she loved that." Kira recalled her animation in the galley afterwards. Had it been anger when she'd assumed it was excitement?

"I don't give a shit," he said. "I'd never do that to you. Don't you know that by now?"

She nodded against his chest, dismayed when her throat clogged. "We have a deal," she murmured.

Jack stiffened and pushed her slightly away. "Damn deal."

"You're unhappy with the deal?"

"I've been unhappy with the deal since we made it."

"Could've fooled me!" Kira spun out of his embrace, hair flying. "You hid your *unhappiness* pretty well in the sack."

Sure he wanted to marry her. *Bite me, Mom.*

"That's not what I meant." He rolled his neck, underlining the tense gesture with a one-handed massage. The other hand gripped her upper arm. "I don't like the terms, which you have a tendency to change willy-nilly."

She drew herself up. "I haven't changed them once." He shot her a look. "Today," she hastily amended.

"Because you're waiting until I've got a hard-on. When I'm weak."

Kira bit her lip to keep a smile at bay. "You're safe tonight. I'll be sleeping blissfully in my childhood bed, one hundred and twenty miles away."

"And I'll be in and out of a cold shower all night." He loosened the death grip on her arm, but pulled her closer, his scent enveloping her and making her head spin. "I'm going to miss you."

And that, ladies and gentlemen was probably as close to a declaration of love as she'd ever get.

"I'm going to miss you too."

"You'll owe me for this."

"Oh no. The bylaws state—"

"To hell with the bylaws." He twirled them around so he was sitting on the hood, and yanked her between his legs. "No more bylaws. No more addendums. No more rules."

"You're such a renegade."

"Just you and me, between the sheets."

"A rebel without a clause."

"Whenever, wherever. No more damn rules."

"Let me think about it—"

His mouth came down near hers and she melted into his body. "No more thinking, either. It's what gets us into trouble."

"Now who's making rules?"

He growled, stepping back and holding out a hand. "Deal?"

They laughed and she shook his hand. "Deal."

Chapter Nine

Moral dilemma number nine –
If you can't hurry love, can you at least clobber it over the head?

The screen door slapped shut as Kira charged into the house. The sound startled her mother, who stood at the kitchen sink, rinsing dishes and loading the dishwasher.

"I want to talk about the yardstick."

"Settle down, Kira." Maggie peered over the top of lime green reading glasses.

Kira joined her at the sink and picked up a handful of silverware. "Tell me about the yardstick called love."

"Oh." Maggie bent to tuck a pot into the bottom rack. Kira handed her the bouquet of silverware and she stowed that too. "This is such an exciting time in your life."

"Cut to the chase, Mom." Kira lifted a butcher knife.

"I remember the butterflies, the anxiety—"

"Mom." She held the knife under the stream of water from the faucet and scraped some crud off with her fingernail.

"Oh all right. I had this speech prepared all your life. Take an old lady's pleasure away."

They laughed. If any fifty-year-old woman could be considered old-ladyish, she certainly wouldn't be Maggie.

"Before I tell you about the yardstick, would you please stop waving that knife around?"

Kira sheepishly dried the knife and slid it into a butcher-block sheath. Maggie poured her a tall glass of iced tea and started scrubbing the counter.

"What I meant by the yardstick is, Jack interferes in your relationships because he loves you and wants the best for you. No one treats you as well as he does and he notices. It's extraordinary."

"Oh Mom," Kira grabbed a towel and stared out the picture window. "I know he loves me. I love him too. That's not the issue." She wiped her hands dry.

"Then what is the issue?"

Taking her iced tea to the table, Kira pulled out a chair and plopped down. "Before the other night, we were like siblings. We got along great—no hassles, no hard feelings. Now we're some weird jumble of…I don't know." How in the world could she explain it to her mother? She couldn't even explain it to herself.

An impish grin grew on Maggie's face. She turned to face Kira and leaned against the counter, arms folded. "Want to tell me how that happened?"

Did she? Kira sighed, running a hand through her hair. Though the admission made her feel trampy, she pressed onward and outlined exactly what had occurred in the cockpit—with a ruthless edit of the kiss—and what had happened since. When she finished, she sat alone at the table, chin on hand, unable to look at her mother.

After a while, Maggie settled down beside her and said, "You know, I really admire you."

Kira's head snapped up and her mother brushed a strand of hair out of her eyes. "You do?"

Maggie nodded. "I wish I'd had the guts to do that with your father. He took forever to ask me out." She gazed wistfully out the window for a long moment, as if willing the lost time to come back.

Grief had etched fine lines around her mouth, on her forehead. Smile lines from so many blissful years with Tom Allen fanned out from intelligent eyes that hadn't accentuated a significant grin in months. Kira's heart grew heavy. "Was it worth it?" she asked.

Maggie frowned and turned enormous eyes on Kira. "Of course it was worth it. Every second."

"I don't remember ever hearing him say he loved you," she said sadly. For that matter, he'd never told her or Mike, either. But they always knew he did.

"Kira." Maggie's soft hand shot out and gripped Kira's. "He told me every day of his life by being a good father and a faithful husband. I didn't need the words. Words are…nothing."

Kira gulped and nodded in half-hearted agreement. Like everyone else in the family, her mother had lived without the words and toed the line, suppressing her own needs in deference to Kira's father's demands. But she'd been happy.

Now Kira was considering the whole hog with Jack—Tom's star pupil. Had she gone mad? There was no way she'd ever suppress her own needs.

But wait.

Jack didn't expect her to. He presented his side of the argument, and though he might moan about it, he acquiesced when she stood her ground.

Jack was so…good to her. He urged her to feel more deeply about everything, made her think about things with a detail she never would've managed on her own.

If she lived to be a hundred and traveled from pole to pole, would she ever find anyone else like him in the world?

In a flash, she knew what had kept her parents together. What could keep her and Jack together despite their differences. There was a name for it too, she thought wryly.

Passionate love.

"Anyway," Maggie said briskly. "You had this layover deal and now Jack wants you to live with him?"

"That's what he says." Taking a sip of iced tea, she tipped her head back and let the trickle of cold liquid soothe her suddenly parched throat.

"He's advancing the relationship."

She shook her head and crunched an ice cube. "He feels badly about my condo."

"It's more than that."

"Do you think he's in love with me?" Mirroring the tinkle of ice in her glass, Kira heard the fragile wistfulness in her own voice, and was about to cringe and crack a joke, but her mother's eyes softened as she reached to finger-comb Kira's hair.

"Honey, he's down for the count."

If only that were true. Tonight, Kira wanted to pretend it was, that this conversation with her mother was for real and that she stood on the brink of all-consuming happiness…

Okay, so she could be girly. Sometimes.

"I'm not sure. He never says anything remotely lover-like. In fact, it's mostly the opposite."

"I didn't say he would admit it."

That put a depressing spin on things. "Do you think he even knows he loves me?"

"No," Maggie said flatly, fanning her palms on the table and inspecting her fingernails.

Kira slumped. "That's just sad."

"It only gets worse from here."

"Oh Mom." She scooted her chair closer and dropped her head into Maggie's lap. "I love him so much it hurts."

"I know, baby. I know." Maggie's cool fingers traced delicate patterns around the shell of her ear. "You've got to remember Jack's history. The boy who came to live with us had a battered spirit. First his mother kicked his father out then she canned him. Jack's come a long way, but I doubt he's going to let himself trust easily."

"How can he not trust me? I've been his best friend for fifteen years."

"It's not you he distrusts, Kira. It's love. Don't you see how he still walks on eggshells around us? Let's us have our way, even if it's not what he wants?"

Kira bolted upright. "So if Dad asked him to marry me, he'd do it?" A quiver of arrows lodged in her heart. If Maggie were correct about the little talk Jack had with Tom, Kira would never be sure of his true feelings for her.

"Good question."

Some help you are. "Do you think that's why he agreed to the layover deal?" She wanted to scream.

"I think it's safe to say he followed his own desires on that one." Maggie laughed gently. "And I somehow doubt he'd go so far as to marry you against his will."

"But how far would he go?" she choked.

"Honey, back up and give him some credit. He's got a good head on his shoulders. That being said, rest assured, he lives in fear that you're going to drop him."

Unable to sit another second, Kira hopped up and started pacing. "It's time for him to stop."

Maggie's intense gaze followed her back and forth like a metronome. "Yes. And you can help him."

"I have no idea how."

"Tell him how you feel."

A bomb could've dropped through the ceiling and caused less damage to her nerves. Every cell in her body screamed in fear at the thought of baring her soul to Jack, watching his eyes go dead.

Oh God. "No way. He'd run like hell."

"He might at first." Maggie chewed the idea like a terrier. "But he'd be back. Trust me. That man craves family more than any man I've ever seen. He just hasn't figured it out yet."

Frozen in the middle of the kitchen, Kira scraped her face and rolled her neck. Great. She was becoming Jack. "I can't handle this."

"Tell you what," Maggie got up and massaged her sore shoulders. "Later we'll make popcorn and watch a movie in bed. I'll scratch your back."

"That's great, Mom, but I'm not ten anymore. You can't make the world go away."

"No. But I can make it a little easier to navigate."

* * * * *

Jack hummed across the Triboro Bridge, stereo blasting, fingers keeping tempo on the steering wheel—

trying to ignore the hollowness of the empty passenger seat.

Kira was his. Yeah! On his terms, no less. He let loose a banshee roar that carried away on the wind, leaving his insides as hollow as the empty passenger seat.

He hated leaving her in Montauk. Felt too far away. What if she needed him? She and Maggie were sitting ducks out there on the tip of the island. Well, they'd handle it, Jack reminded himself. They were capable women.

And therein lay the problem.

What if Kira found out she *didn't* need him? Maggie was there. Mike was on his way. What use would Kira have for Jack now, apart from his penis?

Things can be replaced. People can't.

Maggie's words looped in his brain. Things, as in penises? He cranked the stereo louder.

Things can be replaced. People can't.

You don't have to yell, he thought.

Things can be—

"Wrong," he told Maggie, surprised to find he'd spoken out loud. "People get replaced all the time."

So did penises.

As if to underscore the sentiment, a pudgy, middle-aged man driving the same exact car as Jack roared up beside him and waved.

Bet you and your penis got replaced, buddy. Jack considered popping him the bird. But that seemed even more pathetic than a menopausal man in a hot sports car.

Did Jack look like that?

He stole a glance in the rearview mirror. His sunglasses hid the reflection. Nah. He was still young.

Not for long.

No way was it time to buy a sedan. Then he'd really look established. Like a family man. Jack shuddered. *That's bad?* "Hell yeah," he said out loud again, looking around, like someone on the bridge might have heard him.

It's official, he thought. I'm losing it. It's Kira's fault. Kira the Queen of Disposable Men.

Jack blinked. How many men *had* she gone through before him? She was always chucking them. Sure, he helped from time to time. But mostly, the decision had been Kira's.

Mostly.

And he was next. Already she was separating, staying with Maggie, dragging her feet about living with him.

Funny thing about that. He'd initially asked Kira to live with him as a ruse to distract her, but now he wanted it. He hadn't been lying when he'd said the idea had grown on him. It had. Especially when they'd made love this morning.

He liked waking up next to her, liked eating breakfast with her and liked having her beside him in the passenger seat as well as the cockpit. He just plain old liked being with her. All the time. And he didn't want to be just another penis to her.

When had that happened? They'd always spent loads of time together, but since Tom's last request, Jack had made a point of tying her to him. And as time passed, he'd tightened the knots. Not because he had to, he realized. Because he wanted to.

But Kira had made it abundantly clear she wanted no part of city living. Jack supposed it was her way of rejecting him. Perhaps she thought it softened the blow to say no to New York, not to him directly.

Dandy.

Just what he needed. The minute he got truly interested in a woman, for the first time in his life…

Shit. He knew all along she'd leave him. No sense crying about it now. At least she'd agreed to "no rules" sex until she did. That was something. A small victory to mark in his memoirs.

Wait. She had agreed, hadn't she? Kind of?

This was fucked up.

He pulled out his cell phone and hit number three, Maggie's phone number, on his speed dial. The action reminded him that while Kira was number one on his phone, he wasn't on hers. That rankled. Somehow, some way he had to be number one.

"Hello?" Kira's voice vibrated through the line, straight into his crotch. Jack closed his eyes briefly before remembering the speedometer needle hovered in the ninety mph vicinity.

"Hey."

"Hey yourself. Are you home?"

"Almost. Going to catch a few z's before I go get Mike. Hey. Question. Did you or did you not agree to 'no rules' sex?"

Her soft laughter rippled across his eardrum and made him shiver. "I believe we shook on it."

"Yeah, but you didn't look too thrilled."

"Oh. I have to be thrilled? Aren't you getting kind of grabby there?"

"You think *this* is grabby? You ain't seen nothing yet."

"Don't go making me all wiggly. Mom has a girl's night planned. Are you going out with Mike later?"

Jack smiled at the slight worry in her voice. He should make her sweat. Now's the chance. "No. We'll be up early meeting you in Atlantic Beach, remember?"

She blew out a relieved breath and his heart flip-flopped. She definitely cared about him. No question. So how could he make her care enough to move in?

The answer came to him in a flash. "You know," he said. "Now that we don't have to play by any rules, what do you say we go out on a date?"

There was a shocked silence on the other end.

"Kira? You there?"

"Sorry. I was peeling myself up off the floor. Did you say *date*?"

"Yeah. As in dinners, movies, flowers..." *Me hurling from the anxiety of trying to impress you.*

"You mean romance?"

Jack swallowed. "If you want to call it that."

"Courtship?"

Jack's mouth started watering as his stomach yawed. "Not sure I'd go that far."

"Then what do you mean by 'date'?"

Would it be polite to curse her openly? He could hear the amusement in her voice. "You know. Date."

"Oh I get it. You mean justify the wild sex with dinner first. Make it seem like a real relationship."

"Exactly." That's what he loved about Kira. She always got it. "What do you say?"

"I'll sleep on it."

Jack sagged into the leather seat. The image of her sleeping curled around him. She looked so cute, mouth open, little string of drool oozing out. He always wanted to lick her awake. "Tomorrow night you and Mike trade places. We're going out."

"Might I ask where?" Unmistakable sarcasm in her tone. Jack frowned. Did she not trust him? Guess the Yankee game was out.

Where could he take her that would blow her mind? After scrounging in the ruins, she'd need to get away from it all. The seed of an idea sprouted. "I'm taking you out for lobster."

"Oh goody. I love lobster."

Chest puffed, he said goodnight, circled back through Manhattan and headed out to JFK to arrange everything.

The crew lounge was teeming when he got there. Plenty of people to bullshit with until Mike's plane arrived. Jack made himself at home with a crowd of pilots, and had a grand old time until Arlo came slinking through the door.

"Hello Jack." He smirked. Jack noticed his suit looked starched. Corporate moron. "How's Kira?"

Jack bristled at the sound of her name on the jerk's lips. People like him shouldn't be allowed to talk. "Great."

"Heard her condo got destroyed. I'll have to call and check on her."

"No, you won't," Jack said. "She's not available anymore."

"Says who?"

"Says me."

Arlo's beady eyes measured Jack for a minute. "You boinking her? Isn't that, like, incest?"

Finally. Arlo's true colors emerged. Jack didn't spare himself a congratulatory second. "Watch your mouth."

Arlo shrugged. "Whatever." And slithered off to pester a gaggle of flight attendants.

Jack took a few deep breaths to settle down. There, he'd done it. He'd declared Kira off-limits and by tomorrow, word would be out. No hope of her mating within the ranks of Pan Air anymore.

Damn that felt good. If it hadn't, Jack would've ripped Arlo's lungs out for the boinking comment. But knowing Kira was officially off the market calmed him like a drug. She bore his stamp.

He'd never cared about any woman enough to make sure every man within sniffing distance knew she was his. Kira deserved it though. She was special.

Now if he could only figure out what to do with her.

For the next couple of hours he thought about it while eating dinner and wandering through the airport. No ready answers were forthcoming. He knew he could romance her, spoil her, give her the time of her life. But how in the hell could he keep her when she could have any penis she wanted? Somehow, his penis had to be different.

Indispensable.

He was pacing at the security gate, jingling his keys, when Mike's plane disembarked. There he came, up the concourse to save the day, big-ass grin on his handsome face.

"How the hell have you been?" They embraced in a whopping bear hug, slapping each other's backs and trying not to look *too* happy to see each other. But man it felt good to have Mike here. Jack suddenly realized how much he'd missed his one-man cheering squad. With Tom gone, it was them against the female world.

"I'm great buddy. Great. Flight was excellent. They treated me like the Pope. Where's Kira?"

"With Maggie for the night."

"How's she holding up?"

"So far so good. She's worried about Tom's cockpit case. It was in her office."

Mike fell silent as they walked to the car. No surprise. They all felt the same way about that cockpit case.

"I hope it's okay," Mike said.

"Me too. Look, it's just you and me. You hungry?"

"No. They put me in first class, fed me filet mignon. I think they'd have fed me a stewardess if I wanted one. Who are you, Sultan of Pan Air?"

Jack chuckled. "I've got friends in high places. So how come you didn't let them feed you a stewardess? You sick?" He motioned Mike to the left and they exited the terminal to the parking lot.

"Haven't leaked the news yet, but," Mike smiled and flattened a hand over his heart, "I'm betrothed."

The air got vacuumed out of Jack's lungs. "No shit. I didn't know you had a girlfriend." Mike was getting married? Mike? Married?

"I haven't, for long. Got hit by the thunderbolt."

"When, how, where?"

"Name's Lucy Myers. She's a sculptor in Santa Fe. Met her at a gallery opening couple of months ago."

"Couple of months? Are you crazy?" No one got married after a couple of months. Mike needed some serious head time.

"Hey man. When it's right, it's right."

Jack stared at him as they got into the car. He looked content and relaxed. Unusual for Mike. He also looked happy. Damn. "How well do you know her?"

"Been together twenty-four/seven since we met. We want the same things, you know?"

"Like what?"

"Lots of kids. That sort of thing."

Right. That sort of thing.

What the hell did that mean?

Everyone wanted kids. The problem was staying together to raise them. "How do you know she'll let you raise the kids?"

In the darkness, Mike twisted to watch him. "Because she said *yes*."

"That doesn't mean anything. What if, one day, she kicks you out?"

"That won't happen."

"It could."

"If it does, at least I'll have had her for a while."

Same thing Jack told himself about Kira and the layover deal, but it wasn't enough. At least not for Jack. Not anymore. "I couldn't live like that."

Mike laughed softly. “You already do, buddy. Always waiting for the other shoe to drop.”

Jack opened his mouth to protest but no words came out. Who needed head time now?

“Am I right?” Mike asked.

Hell if he’d say yes.

“Most people don’t act like your mother, Jack. Take my parents—”

“Correction,” Jack said. “Most people *do* act like my mother. Your parents are the exception.” He downshifted and stopped at the parking lot tollbooth.

Mike handed him a fistful of dollars. “You’re probably right. But you got to have hope, man. Without hope, there’s no life.”

“Wrong.” Jack had no hope but he had a life. He had a hell of a life. A fan-flippin’-tastic orgasmatron of a life. And he had Kira to prove it. And this great car. And a glamorous career. And Kira.

A tiny voice in his head admired Mike for taking that leap of faith. *Mike’s brave… Mike’s a true hero.*

How did he find the courage?

“I don’t understand how you get up everyday and go out in the world without that hope,” Mike said.

“That’s because you’re an artist. You’re sensitive.” Jack made it sound like a curse, even though he didn’t think he meant to. “I’m just a shallow SOB.” *And cowardly to boot.*

“Don’t sell yourself short.”

Maybe Mike could give him bravery lessons. “What was it about Lucy that made you go out on a limb?”

"I don't see it that way. But then, you have a point. This is the riskiest thing I've ever done in my life. You, on the other hand, have a risky job. What you need is a safety net at home."

Jack snorted. "Impossible."

"Kira's safe," he offered gently.

"That's what you think."

"Why not marry her? Any idiot can see you're crazy about each other."

Jack waited for a red light to change. Crazy for each other's sex parts was more like it. He floundered to catch his voice. "I'm concentrating on the road."

"Just thought I'd ask."

"And anyway, you and Tom said you'd kill me if I touched her."

Mike laughed his head off. "We had to. You started jerking off the minute you saw her."

"I did not." But it made him chuckle.

They got quiet for a couple of exits. Next thing Jack knew, he was turning down 70th Street on autopilot.

"So you kept a lid on it all these years." Mike broke the silence as they parked and got out. "Remarkable."

Not quite. But Mike didn't need to know that yet. "Tom told me to take care of her, so I became another brother."

"Looks like you did a great job, bro."

"Not really. He wanted me to find her a suitable husband."

"Have you?" Mike smirked knowingly and Jack got a guilty pang in his gut. Why, he didn't know. Did Mike think he'd shirked his duty? Finding someone for Kira was no easy job. Perhaps Mike needed further explanation, so he could fully understand Jack's dilemma.

"So far, only sphincters have applied."

"Thought so."

Jack glanced at him as they crossed the brightly lit, concrete garage to the elevator. The smirk hadn't gone away. Jack got the impression Mike still doubted his sincerity. "I'm trying but she's picky. You know how she is."

"Sure do."

"I help her screen potentials." He punched the elevator button.

Mike nodded.

Jack sighed. "We just can't agree on anyone."

"Not surprising."

"Why's that?"

"Because you were meant for each other, lamebrain. No one else is ever going to be good enough."

"Tom didn't think I was good enough," Jack countered. "He asked me to—"

"I know what he asked you to do. Which is strange because it's not what he said to me."

"And that was?" The elevator doors slid open and they stepped inside.

"He wanted Kira to marry *you*."

Chapter Ten

Moral dilemma number ten –
If you heard one thing, and someone else heard another, can you twist things to suit your purposes?

Jack's entire body iced over in shock. Like in the stupid television cartoons he'd watched as a kid he could feel hairline cracks spoking outward from his chest, snapping through his arms and speeding down his legs. In a minute, he'd be lying on the ground in a pile of shattered chunks. The old man *wanted* him to be Kira's husband? Why? He'd been a giant fuck-up for most of his life. Maybe he'd redeemed himself a little by the end, but it was still a major stretch for the old man to have had such faith in him. Jack simply wasn't worthy. Was he?

"What?" The word echoed around the parking garage.

"The old man never said anything to you about that?"

"No!" This was bullshit. There was no chance in hell Tom sincerely believed Jack would make his *daughter* a good husband. No man in his right mind would want Jack anywhere near his daughter. Or anyone else's for that matter. The cancer must've eaten more than the poor guy's liver.

But Mike never lied.

A tiny spark of truth ignited inside and tentative pride huffed and puffed in his lungs. Mike was more honest than a priest.

"Man. Those last hours, that's all he talked about. Ticked me off big-time and made me feel unloved. Then I realized it was because you guys had unfinished business. He was trying to tie up all the loose ends before he went."

Jack had trouble breathing. "A giant among men."

"Tell me about it."

While Mike stared at the lights over the elevator doors, Jack gnawed on the information. Kira and Mike were both at Tom's side when he died. She must have heard what he'd said. Yet, she'd never mentioned it. Why? *Because she doesn't want to marry you, dickweed.* His stomach knotted. Not that he wanted to marry her either. He didn't want to marry anyone, ever. Especially not Kira. He'd be too happy. Then she'd leave.

However, if Tom asked him to… Jack mentally shook his head. Tom hadn't asked. Instead he'd instructed Jack to take care of her and *find her a husband*.

Had that been a cryptic message?

All these months Jack had taken his mission so seriously, felt so trapped by the responsibility of it and so anxious to be free, he'd never stopped to consider Tom's motivation. Had he been trying to thrust them together, hoping they'd fall in love? What a laugh. Tom knew better than anyone that Jack would never let himself fall in love. They'd talked about it.

So why did he say that to Mike?

They arrived at his door, carried the suitcases in and Jack realized his sofa was still strewn with bedding from last night.

"You have company?" Mike asked, dropping his duffel bag beside an easy chair and sinking into it. He bent to remove his shoes, tossing them aside and digging bare toes into the thick carpet and sitting back with a contented sigh.

"Kira stayed here last night," Jack said. Mike raised an eyebrow and Jack had the sickening feeling it was time to come clean. Mike would find out tomorrow anyway. "We hooked up a couple of days ago."

Mike blinked and Jack turned away, hurrying into the kitchen for a cold beer. Why he felt so embarrassed over this, he had no idea. But there it was.

Didn't take long for Mike to appear behind him. Jack buried his head in the fridge. Mike tapped him on the shoulder.

"S'cuse me. What did you just say?"

Showtime. Jack straightened, shoving a bottle into Mike's hand. "I said we're together."

"Together together?"

Jack took a swig and nodded, hoping he wouldn't be required to provide details. How could he explain to her brother that it started out as a fling without sounding like a dime store lothario? Never mind it had grown and developed and now he planned on actually dating her. It wasn't as if it was going to lead anywhere.

Mike didn't seem to care either way. "Holy shit that's great!" He pumped Jack's hand. "That's great buddy. Why didn't you tell me before?" He rocked back on his heels, surveying Jack with a sense of wonder in his eyes.

"I was shy," Jack said and allowed an ironic grin.

"You were scared."

"That too."

They guffawed and Mike clinked the bottles in toast. "To the happy couple."

Right. Happy couple.

* * * * *

By the time Kira and Maggie arrived in Atlantic Beach the next day, Jack and Mike were standing at the orange and white striped sawhorses blocking her street, chatting with two police officers.

Hair glistening from the shower, Jack looked awesomely fresh and masculine in a loose T-shirt and gym shorts. And there was Mike, golden haired and tall, dressed in surfer shorts and a mesh muscle shirt.

As they climbed out of the car and walked over, Kira peered beyond the men at the mess her street had become. Sand dunes buttressed the brick walls of the condo complexes. Cars had been swept up and deposited helter-skelter. Heaps of beach debris lay everywhere.

She searched for her red Mini Cooper in the parking lot, and spotted it wedged between a dumpster and a green SUV. A chalky coating of salt marred the gleaming new surface. Tears sprang into her eyes just as Mike spied her and jogged over.

"Hey kiddo." He swept both the women into a tight embrace and through a haze of bittersweet joy, Kira noticed Jack hovering on the sidelines, as if hesitant to join them.

"Jack?" She broke away from Mike and threw herself into his arms. He took her in, holding her head against his strong, warm shoulder. She buried her nose in his neck, inhaling deeply and needing him more than she ever thought possible. "I missed you."

"I missed you too," he murmured.

"I'm so glad you're here." Nestled in the welcoming cocoon of Jack's body, a refreshing vigor spread through her, as if she'd landed on solid ground after a hair-raising flight. She wished they could stay like this forever.

"I told Mike about us." Jack spoke into her ear, so no one else could hear. "I also told that prick Arlo."

Kira lifted her face. "You did?" He was spreading the news around Pan Air, staking a claim. He'd asked her out on a "date". Normally she would've been thrilled by all these developments, but today she wondered why. Did he intend carrying out her dad's last request by proposing? Forget it if he did. No way was she going to marry Jack because he owed some dysfunctional debt to Tom. It was passionate love, or nothing.

Jack planted a kiss on her nose. "No sense keeping it secret, since we're officially hooked up."

Ever the romantic.

"Mom knows too. She had some rather interesting insights," Kira said.

"Funny. So did Mike."

They stared at each other, each seeming to will the other to expand.

"Somebody call?" Mike ambled over with a grin. "You got lucky, Sis. The cops said in most cases so far, the damage looks worse than it is. Apparently, the waves made it as far as the building, but didn't undermine the structure. The stockade fence around the parking lot acted as a buffer. There's probably some leakage inside your unit, but it should be relatively minor."

Relative to what? Kira wiped her damp brow.

"That's the good news," Jack said. "Unfortunately, your car took a beating. I called the insurance company and they'll send someone out today or tomorrow." He squeezed her shoulders as she slumped against him.

"Shall we sally forth into the wreckage?" Mike asked.

Lifting her chin, Kira said, "Let's roll." And prepared herself for the worst, despite what Mike had said.

As a group they crossed through the police blockade, sidestepping driftwood, splintered tree branches and garbage cans. Kira paused beside her car, silently acknowledging the water damage and assuming it would be totaled out by insurance. Well, as much as she liked the red Mini, maybe her next one would be yellow. The idea shored her up enough to unlock the front door of her condo and put one tentative foot inside.

Water pooled around her footprint in the area rug. Kira lifted her foot out of the puddle and the water promptly disappeared as if sucked into a dry sponge, but not before a baby sand crab skittered across her sneaker.

Not a good sign.

Stepping further in, followed closely by Jack and the rest, she shot a hasty glance around the room and felt her spirits sink. Damp beach sand swirled across the buckling wood floors of the living room, and seaweed hung in glistening clumps around the legs of her dining room chairs.

"Not bad," Jack said. "A little elbow grease and a wet/dry vac should do it."

"You think?" Kira's knees went out so she flopped onto the sofa, only to jump up with a yelp and a cold, soggy behind.

"Oh my," Maggie said.

"This bites," Mike said.

Rust colored water stains crawled halfway up the warm yellow walls and as Kira sucked air in distress, the dank odor of mildew and dead sea creatures assailed her nose.

"It chews cud all right," Jack said, apparently giving up his bid to be optimistic.

"And spits it out," Kira added.

"I think everything but the rugs, furniture, flooring and walls survived just fine," Maggie said, clasping her hands together and bringing them to her lips.

They all froze, looked at her, and made a beeline for Kira's office.

Her hand hovered over her heart as Jack sloshed across the tiny room and returned bearing the cockpit case, unscathed. He opened it and they gathered round to peer inside. The musty odor of world travel wafted up to greet them. Mike let loose a coyote-howl of triumph and, except for Kira, they all relaxed, somber moods changing to cautious happiness like someone had flicked a switch.

"See? Everything's okay," Maggie said, wandering over to Kira's vintage steel desk and poking around in the papers.

Kira slanted her a frown. She would never understand her mother's capacity for denial.

"Don't look at me that way, Kira," Maggie said. "Someone's got to accentuate the positive. All our family treasures survived." She fingered the blue wool Pan Air blanket suspended on the citrus orange wall behind Kira's desk. "And that's something to grab onto."

"Easy for you to say. All my other stuff is landfill fodder." Kira sat down in her vintage wooden desk chair, running tender hands along the time-smoothened armrests. She'd found this chair on the side of the road, on big trash collection day out in Bayshore. Now it had scum hanging from the legs.

When she went to stand up again, her feet crunched in the sand, making her wince for the parquet floor she'd so lovingly restored.

Dammit. She didn't deserve this, even if she did want to live where nature didn't want her. She fired an accusing glance at Jack, as if his strictures had caused this to happen.

He blinked. "What?"

"Nothing," she snapped, feeling lousy for blaming him, but continuing to do it just the same.

Maggie clapped her hands, drawing everyone's attention away from the devastation. "Kira and I packed up a hamper of bagels, cream cheese and coffee. Who's hungry?"

Okaaay. Her mother's forced chirpiness was seriously irritating her. "Not to change the subject, Mom. But what am I going to do?" Kira wailed. "I'm glad Dad's mementos survived. But look at this mess." She threw out her arms and came into abrupt contact with Jack's rock-solid chest.

Jack nudged her with his shoulder, the brief skin-on-skin contact of their arms a soothing reminder of what he meant to her. "Replace everything," he said.

"No!" Kira cried. "I don't want to replace my things. I love them." She turned defiantly and surprised an odd expression on his face. "What?"

He shook his head, blue eyes growing large, dark and luminous as he gazed at her. "I should've known you'd feel that way."

It made her shiver, the look in his eyes. "Well," she stuttered. "Of course I do. When have you known me to throw anything out?"

Sorry, but despite what his tender expression was doing to her body, his comment pissed her off. Jack should know by now that when she committed to owning something, she loved it forever. Cleaning this place out was going to be hell.

* * * * *

Jack felt like a kid who'd heard Santa's sleigh bells in the night. He'd been an ass.

As the women set out the picnic brunch, and he and Mike cleared seaweed off the chairs and wiped down the table, the hard shell around his heart cracked and began to chip away like candy coating off an ice cream bar.

Why hadn't he seen it before?

Without a word, Maggie handed him plastic silverware and napkins while Kira piled a plate with his favorite—an onion bagel and gobs of cream cheese. Mike stirred cream into his coffee exactly the way he liked it and handed him the foam cup like he'd done plenty of times over the years.

"Oh, I forgot the raspberry jelly." Maggie placed a warm hand on Jack's arm. "I'm sorry, sweetheart. We rushed out the door this morning and I forgot."

"It's gross, anyway," Mike commented. "I'm glad I don't have to watch him scarf that crap."

"I've got some." Kira brushed past Jack and into the kitchen, reappearing with the jar she'd bought especially for him.

What a dolt he'd been.

Like a well-rehearsed ballet, they took the same seats they'd always taken during the countless meals they'd shared. Mike across the way, Maggie at the head of the table, and Kira to his left. He gazed at her affectionately and realized the erection swelling in his shorts didn't come from her blonde beauty, or her delicious scent or the way she blew his mind in bed. It came from the clot of emotion clinging to his innards.

His buddy Kira didn't throw things, or people away. Ergo, she'd never ditch Jack. And neither would Maggie or Mike.

Adopted or not, Jack was part of their family. For keeps.

It galled him a little that Mike had been right, but for now he felt too happy to care.

Grinning like an idiot, he took a huge bite out of his bagel and listened to *his* family chatter. Even through sea-salted windows, the sun streaming in somehow seemed brighter than it ever had before.

"You can collect the insurance money and Jack and I will do the work," Mike was saying to Kira. "Buy me a honeymoon with the leftover cash."

It took a moment of stunned silence for his statement to sink in. When it did, the women exploded.

Jack leaned back on the chair legs, thumbs hooked in waistband, listening to Mike reiterate the engagement story. Somehow, the brevity of it seemed more plausible today than it had late last night, when he was tired and aching for Kira.

He glanced at her. Hell. Any man would fall for her hard and fast. Wouldn't even take as long as it took Mike to fall for Lucy. He smirked victoriously, knowing he'd gotten the better deal.

Wait.

There was no more deal.

Jack's chair came crashing down, startling everyone. Just because she wouldn't toss him out with the trash didn't mean she'd continue to need his penis forever—especially not without a *bona fide* deal. But he'd nixed the deal, dammit. Now he had to think up a new one and think it up quick.

A light bulb flashed over his head.

Forget dating. Dating was for sissies. He would go for broke and marry her.

Did he want to marry her?

In a dazzling white brain detonation, he realized he did. What better way to take care of her, keep her close, and have earth-shattering sex for the rest of his life?

Problem. She didn't want to marry him.

Solution! He'd reiterate Tom's last request, make her realize Tom had their best interests at heart, that he knew what they needed from life and from each other.

Kira'd see the sense in that.

What about love?

What about it?

Being in love was fraught with danger. But being part of the Allen family, now that was safety incarnate.

Kira and Jack were buddies. Best friends. They enjoyed each other's company and had mind-boggling sex together. What stronger foundation for marriage could there be?

Don't you want her to love you? the pesky voice whined. Not on your life, Jack answered. He wanted to be indispensable, not loved. With a marriage license in hand, that's exactly what he'd be. But only with Kira, because she *stayed.*

Tonight, in Bar Harbor, he'd make love to her like never before, make her silly, stupid and weepy. And he'd propose. No way would she be able to say no.

Brilliant plan. Infallible. Jack congratulated himself.

Chapter Eleven

Moral dilemma number eleven –
Is it better to save face on the blade of a katana, or run away?

After the leisurely brunch, they all decided there wasn't any point in sticking around the condo, so Kira rooted through the top drawers of her bureau for undamaged clothing. Thank God most of her expensive outfits, as well as her work uniforms, had been on hangers in the closet, suspended safely above the seeping destruction. She kept an ice-blue sheath she intended wearing tonight on a hanger covered in plastic, and folded the rest into black garbage bags.

The entire time, Jack's demeanor worried her. He'd adopted a hazy expression and a mild, cooperative attitude. Not once did an insult or scathing tease pass his sexy lips and he downright refused to be drawn into a sparring match. And she itched for one, big and bad.

She realized their banter turned her on, made her feel safe and secure and hot as all get out. This new Jack irritated her beyond belief.

You got what you asked for.

No she didn't. While she yearned for pillow talk with Jack, she didn't necessarily want him to be so agreeable, and unlike the cocky, smartass pilot she adored. Was it all part of his master plan to court her? He couldn't be that dumb, thinking she'd fall for such a phony act. Kira rejected the very idea. Maggie had said he wouldn't leap into marriage just because Tom asked and Kira agreed.

And speaking of that, what had Tom been thinking? He should've known better than to ask that of Jack. Anger tightened her chest for the first time since her father had died. How dare he manipulate her love life from the grave, as if she were too stupid to know her own mind. She appreciated what he'd tried to do, but come on! As if you could make two people fall in love.

Well, he'd accomplished half of that, she thought dismally. She had fallen. Hard. The problem lay in convincing Jack he felt the same way. She sighed.

The morning had progressed into early afternoon by the time Maggie said, "I guess we'll be scooting home." She came up to Kira for a hug. Mike hovered behind, waiting his turn.

"Thanks so much for coming out to help. I'll see you tomorrow." While she was thrilled about Mike's newfound happiness, at the same time her heart ached for requited love with Jack. Mike had met Lucy eight weeks ago, and knew with rock-solid certainty she was the woman for him. Kira and Jack had been together fifteen years. Talk about a late bloomer. Perhaps it was time to quit hoping.

Tell him how you feel. Maggie's words looped in her brain and fear gripped her once again. *He's down for the count.*

Not likely. If it hadn't happened yet, it never would. Confessing her love would probably result in awkward silence on his part, then a stumbling discourse on how much he cared for her, how much fun he'd had with her body, blah, blah. She couldn't and wouldn't tolerate such a dehumanizing scene. She still had some pride.

Yet, a small seed of hope remained, refusing to die and let her have peace. She felt certain the hot light that had engulfed his eyes this morning in her office had been the catalyst for his out-of-character behavior this afternoon. Something between them had changed during the debate over her furniture, and it went deeper than mere sex. No one illuminated from within like that over an unemotional orgasm. She knew that well enough from her own experience.

If only she could get him to admit it.

Desire pooled in her belly as he wedged his athletic body beside hers on the threshold and waved a cheerful goodbye to Maggie and Mike. If, by some miracle, he had fallen in love with her and this cozy domestic scene was an example of what lay ahead for them, she'd keep trying until she died.

"Let's get a move on." He planted a kiss on her forehead and turned to hoist the garbage bag full of clothes. "I want to be on the road by five."

His restiveness had returned. Kira felt cheered when he strode off to his car, in a hurry, as always. After locking the condo, she trailed him, blood heating at the elegant ripple of muscle as he stowed her bag, unlocked the passenger door and leaned back against the car to watch her approach.

His admiring gaze flickered around her body like a hot, lapping tongue, making her ultra-conscious of the way her crotch rubbed against the thick middle seam of her navy shorts. Already, the heat of the midday sun sent a tickle of perspiration down the hollow between her breasts and she wanted to keep moving, straight into him, and do a mamba up against the car.

"Isn't that early?" They still had plenty of time, but they'd have to shower and dress, and the simple trip across the street had primed her for nookie. More than that, she hoped to ruffle him up, make him lose control. Make him confess.

"I need to make a pit stop on the way," he said mysteriously, ushering her into the car and jogging round to the other side. Since he didn't expand, Kira let it drop. Maybe they'd run out of condoms.

During the ride back he seemed quiet and contemplative, though he betrayed his outer calm by zipping in and out of traffic full throttle. "Where's the fire?" she asked flirtatiously. She loved driving fast with Jack. Hell, she loved doing anything with Jack, but she especially loved watching his hands on the wheel, or at the controls of a jet.

He tossed her a smile. "It's a big night. Don't want to be late for our first date."

Warmed by the heat she sensed behind his sunglasses, she smiled back. "So this is a real date, then. Not just an excuse for wild sex."

"Oh it's an excuse for wild sex," he said, sliding a hand between her thighs. "But there's something I want to talk about too."

He wanted to talk? Kira pressed her thighs together, trapping his hand. He wiggled his fingers and yelped in mock protest, making her laugh out loud. He grinned and accelerated to warp speed.

Soon, they were laughing and stumbling noisily into his condo. The door slammed behind them with a satisfyingly private bang, and Jack swept her screaming into his arms and deposited her on the bed.

Kira wiggled joyfully underneath him as he hovered above, smelling wind-whipped and rugged and so much like Jack. When he eased his body down, her eyes rolled back in pleasure. She'd only been away from him a few hours, but she craved him like an addict.

"Let's make love," she whispered.

"Not yet." He licked her lips and brushed his erection over her thighs, taunting her with the drug she so desperately needed. "You're going to get up, get in the shower, dress and go out with me."

"No," she protested, voice achy with sexual hunger. "Don't do this to me."

"Do what?" he intoned. "I'm just laying here."

"Laying being the operative word," she managed.

He pulled away and she pulled him back by his hair. "Jack, I need you."

"I need you too," he said. "But first, the date."

From the depths of her soul rose a groan so potent, she felt the vibration in places she didn't know existed. Her eyelids fluttered shut. "I don't want the date. I want you."

"You have me," Jack stated.

She looked at him. There it was, on his face and in his eyes, everything she'd been hoping to see from the start. A flood of tenderness washed through her, filling her and spilling out from the corners of her eyes.

"You have me too. Always," she whispered.

"And all ways," he said, running a finger down her cheek. "Now get ready."

Keeping her gaze glued to his face, she scooted out from underneath, suddenly famished for this date and the conversation they would have. She felt certain tonight would be the night he declared his love. It was all over him, so aromatic she could smell it, and so spicy her mouth watered.

Lying on his back, arms pillowing his head, he watched her while she undressed. The intense, hot focus of his enlarged pupils kept her mesmerized as she slowly unzipped her shorts and inched them down undulating hips.

"Join me in the shower?" she asked, slipping the sleeves of her tank top down over her arms and removing the top the same way she did the shorts.

"I didn't intend to," he said slowly, gaze riveted on her face. "But I think I've changed my mind."

Kira ran the tip of her tongue across her top lip and Jack pounced, grabbing her hand and pulling her into the bathroom. While the water heated, she undressed him, flicking her tongue over each newly exposed piece of flesh and feeling him quiver with delight.

"I love this with you," he groaned and her lungs seized. So close, and yet so far from a real declaration. *Say it Jack. I know you want to. I know you feel it. Just say it.*

"We're perfect together," she hinted.

"Better than perfect." Opening the frosted glass shower door, he led her inside. As their lips met and devoured in hot, open kisses, steaming spray sluiced their faces, the fresh flavor of the water mingling with the taste of Jack's mouth. Kira pressed hard against him and his hands hydroplaned down her back to her bottom then he sought out the soap and started slicking her up.

First her back, then her stomach and breasts. Kira watched as the suds dribbled along her skin like beach foam at the shore. Jack was the picture of concentration as he lowered to his knees in front of her, slipping a soapy hand up each thigh and letting his fingers linger gently on her labia. His gaze ate up every centimeter of her body as he slowly stood and started shampooing her hair.

A low moan escaped her as his fingertips gripped her scalp, massaging with deliberate thoroughness until every last drop of tension had ebbed away. Then, with one hand in her hair, he used the other to lift her leg around his hip. Kira wound it around him, gasping when he parted her folds and slipped his cock easily inside. Now both hands returned to her hair, raking the slick strands in tandem with his thrusts. Having his hands controlling the movement of her head while their bodies melded with exquisite freedom sent a powerful, erotic surge coursing through her and curled her toes as she braced her free foot on the textured surface of the tub floor. Every cell in her system concentrated on the areas where they joined, at the head and at the hips, brewing an intoxicating concoction in her blood and making her nerves sing in unbearable enjoyment.

Simultaneously, they began pumping each other faster. Kira opened her eyes to see Jack's gaze thumbtacked to hers. She met his gaze levelly and unwavering as they spiraled up to the crest and punched through all restraint, falling apart in each other's arms as genuine, heartfelt orgasms rocked their world.

* * * * *

"Why are we headed inside the airport?" Kira asked later, from the passenger seat of Jack's car. After slipping into the ice-blue sheath, she'd chosen a tightly slicked back messy-bun for her hair. At the last minute, she'd secured a blue topaz cat collar choker around her neck and when she'd emerged from the bathroom, Jack had had to sit down. She'd nearly been knocked over herself by the sight of him in a charcoal gray suit, casually matched with a snug black T-shirt.

The combination of the daring outfit with his chiseled good looks brought to mind an image of awards night in Hollywood and made her realize she hadn't seen him in killer civvies since the senior prom.

"I lost something there last night," he said.

"It's that important?"

"Oh yeah. It's that important."

Okaaay. Curiosity consumed her.

They parked in the short-term lot and crossed the multi-lane demolition derby JFK airport architects considered a road. Inside the terminal, Jack pulled her up short and glanced around as if lost.

"What's wrong?"

"I'm not sure." He pressed a finger to his lips and dug around in his breast pocket, withdrawing a sheaf of paper and handing it to her. "Will you take a look at this and see where we are?"

Had he lost his mind? She glared at him, hand on hip. He pressed the papers into her other hand and she took them begrudgingly, giving them a cursory glance before doing a double take. "These are tickets."

"They are?" Jack moved closer and looked over her shoulder.

"To Maine. Jack. These are tickets to—" Lobster. He was taking her to *Maine* for lobster. "Jack?" Her eyes swam as she looked up to a big-ass grin, and her ability to speak vanished. Never in her life had a man made such a grand gesture, and to have it come from Jack…

She was floored.

"I wanted to take you out for Chinese in Hong Kong, but I figured with Mike here, that'd be rude."

He loved her. He had to. Otherwise why go to these extremes? Thank God she'd been struck dumb because she would've told him how she felt. On the spot. Would've scrambled up on a plastic airport seat and shouted it from the top of her lungs. But she needed to hear it from him first. Had to be rock-solid certain he wasn't messing with her again.

So from somewhere down deep, she dredged up the strength to maintain her composure. Even though inside she was a quivering wreck.

"This is wonderful." Did she say that? It didn't sound like her—this husky, emotional tone.

"Next time," he promised.

"No really. I couldn't be more surprised or pleased, Jack. You outdid yourself."

He rocked back on his heels proudly. "No sense crawling downtown to some crusty crab shack when the world is ours to command. We're going to be doing things like this a lot."

She smiled through a film of tears. "Sounds great."

"Come on, we're at gate thirty-two."

* * * * *

Good God she was stunning, Jack thought as they strolled down the concourse, everything he wanted all wrapped up in a sexy, sweet-smelling package. No wonder he was slobbering all over himself, barely able to hold a thought in his head. He had no doubt he could convince her to marry him, either, not after today in the shower.

He could tell by her face she was falling for him. He just needed to give her that little extra shove. Tom's wish for them to be married would be just the ticket. Kira wanted to please the old man as much as he did.

After they checked in, she ducked into the restroom and he pulled the pale blue jewelry box from his coat pocket. It'd been dicey, but a discreet phone call while she dressed for dinner had resulted in a messenger bringing a small array of rings to the lobby for him to select— bless NYC and its services.

He'd chosen a half-carat marquis that he thought would compliment the delicate bones of her hand. Now he couldn't wait to give it to her. While he paced outside the ladies room, he tried to think of the most romantic way possible to propose.

A click of heels behind made him turn. There she came, hot and succulent. Mike's wise words scrolled in his brain. *Any idiot can see you're crazy about each other.* Jack had to face facts and come clean. He was crazy about Kira. He wanted her, needed her. Funny how that didn't scare him anymore, now that he knew how to become indispensable to her. In a few months, maybe sooner, he'd be her husband, and she'd be stuck. Whoa. His head was about to explode.

"Miss me?" She pulled up beside him and his chest swelled as every male head at gate thirty-two turned to watch. Damn she was cute. It made him smile just thinking about her.

"Every second you're gone," he said, surprised how true those smart-aleck words rang.

Hard to believe he'd even contemplated letting her go. No way could he ever live without Kira. She was the best damn thing that'd happened to him in his crazy, mixed-up life.

And he'd been given the secret to keeping her.

Note to self—pour a case of beer over Tom's grave. Silly maybe, but the old man deserved some recognition. Mike would be glad to oblige.

By the time the plane touched down in Portland and they drove to the restaurant, the last shred of daylight faded to black. They were seated on an outer deck decorated with lighted glass fishing net bobs, and colorfully painted lobster traps.

As they placed their meal order, Jack's stomach pitched and yawed. What was he going to say? How was he going to propose? Every time he met her gaze, or their hands brushed, or his leg found hers under the table, his innards liquefied.

He tried reminding himself this was Kira, his best friend, his lover, but the fear that he might somehow disappoint her seized the words. Maybe if he treated this like an FAA inspection, as if his commercial license could be toasted by some tiny miscalculation.

There was something he could relate to. His inner autopilot switched on. He could do this—logically, coolly and professionally—the same way he passed his six-month checks.

How could she say no?

* * * * *

"Are you nuts?" Later, on the beach, Kira's screech hit his face with the sting of an angry squall. "I'm not going to marry you because daddy said so," she spat. "We're grown-ups, for God's sake and I can't even believe you'd ask."

Jack stared at her, mouth opening and closing like a dying fish. He had scarcely begun his little speech about Tom's last request, hadn't even asked her to marry him or shown her the ring, and immediately she'd torn her hand out of his and pinned him with eyes green and stormy as the sea.

"I didn't ask," he said. Never mind that he'd been about to, that his knuckles felt white as he clutched the blue box in his pocket. Pride had swelled into a shelter from the savagery in her anger, making him glad she'd lashed out before he'd laid his suddenly raw heart at her feet.

"You were about to," she said, kicking sand into the surf. "At first, I thought this might happen." She fell silent for a moment, staring at the waves. Then the face she turned on him wore an expression of disappointment he'd never before seen. "But after I thought about it, I gave you credit for being smarter than that."

"Smarter than what?" Had he been a moron—to think Tom was right, that they should be married, that they'd be happy together, and safe?

"Smarter than any idiot off the street who'd get married because a parent asked them to," she shouted, her face a portrait of misery. "What about love?"

"What about it? You think love is a good reason to get married?" He almost laughed. As if a thin emotion could carry the weight of a lifetime commitment. What he felt for

Kira was far sturdier than mere love—he felt a kinship, that he was necessary, wanted, indispensable. Or he had. Until now.

"It's the only reason," she cried. "Books are written about love, lives lost for it. It's the most important emotion in existence."

"Also the most fragile," he said.

"It's precious," she said.

"It breaks." He strode down the beach, away from her and her disillusionment. He'd displeased her and now she was hurt. Jack's head spun from the pain reflected in her eyes. It went straight to that place he'd armored like a vault. The place where his mother lived, in all her unhappy glory. The place he'd sent her by being a pain in the ass.

He heard Kira scrambling behind in her bare feet, sandals thunking in her hand as she struggled to keep up. The bitter salt of the sea spray stung his lips and nostrils, clouding his vision and giving him a welcome distraction from the explosion of misery in his soul.

Gasping from the sprint, she grabbed his arm. "It doesn't have to break, Jack. Not if it's tended properly."

"Right," he said, gallantry returning as he helped her steady herself in the surf.

"Is it because of your mother that you feel this way?"

"Partly. But you're not exactly known for your long-term relationships." Before the words were out, he regretted them. If he'd taken both fists to her with all his might, she couldn't have looked more battered.

She did, however, recover quickly. "And you are? You're a fine one to talk!"

"Let's not go there."

"Why, because you might actually learn something about yourself?"

No. Because he might learn something about Kira. "I already know enough."

"Not enough to see that you're the one sabotaging my relationships."

His turn to feel sucker-punched. Only this time, it was because her words rang true. Mentally, he replayed the past year, going over each of her relationships in fast-forward. Rob, Tim, Joe. *Arlo.* Every one of the jerks feeling the business end of his boot.

Kira put a hand on his arm. "Mom thinks you do it because you love me."

Her statement galvanized him. "Love is all well and good, Kira, but it's not enough." Her hand dropped away. "What you and I have is better. Stronger. We share a history, things in common, we enjoy each other's company and have a great time in bed."

She nodded. That was good.

Maybe he was breaking through. "We don't have to live in the city full-time. We can use your place as a weekend retreat."

Mediocre reaction, but he could work on it.

"We depend on each other, need each other, we stick by each other through thick and thin."

Vigorous nod.

"We're indispensable to each other."

After a moment, she said, "And?"

He cast around desperately for more reasons to get married. "We both like kids," he said weakly.

She held up a hand. "I've heard enough."

Jack slumped in relief and reached for her but she shrugged off his hand. Arms wrapped around slender waist, she shivered in the late evening breeze, silky dress billowing around her legs and turning his thoughts to bedtime.

When she finally spoke, her voice sounded tiny and far away. "Do you love me?"

Back to that. Shoot an arrow into my heart, why don't you, he thought, agony searing him. Of course he loved her. He'd always loved her. Right from the first moment he saw her standing in the driveway. When Mike and he had ridden their bikes to her house for the very first time. She'd had all the gangly arms, legs and braces of a thirteen-year-old, bearing little indication of the stunner she'd become.

He clearly recalled how she'd made a big deal over his new silver racing bike, practically shoving him off the seat so she could take it for a spin. He'd known then she was his type of girl, and the years, and the layover, had confirmed it.

Lost in reverie, he didn't realize she'd put her own spin on his silence. "Fine."

In a blink she'd spun away and started trotting back toward the restaurant. "Kira! Wait." He took off after her, pumping air and gaining ground until his bare foot bore down on a broken clamshell and started gushing blood hell for leather.

In the few minutes it took to wrap a hankie around his foot, she'd disappeared. Jack slipped into his shoes and limped to the reception desk. "Did you see a tall blonde go out the door?" he asked the mousy hostess.

"Miss Allen? I called her a cab."

Jack pounded a fist on the desk, startling the glasses off the hostess' nose. "Sorry. Look. Any idea where she went?"

"I'm not sure I should say," she snipped, ripping him up and down with her eyes. "The poor woman was crying."

Jack closed his eyes tightly and wrung the back of his neck with a shaky hand. Great. He'd made her cry. She thought he didn't love her when he did. Desperately.

Sitting down on the leather bench beside the desk, he rubbed his face in his hands. God he loved her. Why couldn't he see it before now, in time to squeeze the hell out of her and reassure her? Because you're a dumbass, he told himself. *You don't deserve her. You're too moronic to breathe air.*

He was so totally and completely in love with Kira he couldn't think straight enough to realize it. And it wasn't that intense love that made her run away, it was his refusal to feel it.

Talk about abject failure.

"We had a disagreement," he told the hostess. "I was an ass."

"Typical," she muttered, bringing his head around sharply.

"I have to know where she went. I need to apologize." When the coldhearted girl didn't say anything, he withdrew the ring from his pocket. "I need to give this to her and tell her I'll spend the rest of my life making up for tonight. Please." His hand trembled as he held out the ring and the twit's composure snapped like a twig.

"She went to the airport."

Jack's eyes started burning. To cover himself, he reached for his wallet and threw a couple hundred bucks on the desk. "Have a surf and turf dinner. On me." And he was out the door.

Chapter Twelve

Moral dilemma number twelve –
Where do my needs end and the other person's begin?

By the time she got to the airport, Kira's face was cried clean of makeup. She could feel the puffy scratchiness around her eyes and sinuses. Her entire body thrummed with a hurt so powerful she scarcely thought she'd survive.

Jack didn't love her. Or if he did, it was buried so deep in the pain of his past he wouldn't recognize it if it rose up and bit him.

She wanted to clobber Mrs. Grayson for doing this to an innocent boy. She also wanted to clobber Jack and tell him to get over it. There came a time in every child's life when they had to move forward from their parents' mistakes. She had. Why couldn't Jack?

As much as she ached with love for him, she couldn't live with a man who could never speak the words, or acknowledge the feelings she so desperately needed returned.

They were done for.

Standing forlornly inside the sliding glass doors near the ticket area, she dug around in her little purse, thankful Jack had given her the tickets. She hastily checked the departure board, spotted two flights leaving in an hour, and considered her options.

Should she make Jack find his own way home? He could piggyback in someone's jump seat, or drive and suffer all night.

Or, she could be ladylike and leave his ticket with the agent. He'd be smart enough to check for it and she knew he had his ID tucked safely in his wallet.

In the end, graciousness won and she left the ticket for him to sniff out. As she headed for the gate, boarding pass in hand, she felt good about that decision. The last thing she wanted to be was vindictive and bitter. She did love him, after all.

A quick stop at the gourmet coffee stand helped shore her reserves. Approaching the gate, she noticed the flight crew had arrived and were milling around the jetway ramp door.

By unbelievable coincidence, she spied a familiar French twist of flaming hair. Lea! Kira almost fainted with gratitude for the bestowal of this one small blessing. At least now she'd have someone to commiserate with on the flight back, and maybe she could pinch a ride and flop at Lea's condo in Long Beach—if it was still there. And dry.

"Wait!" Kira called, as Lea, meticulously made-up as usual, stepped through the door.

Lea took a step backward and turned, vivid blue eyes blank at first, then beaming with surprised recognition. "Kira? What the hell are you doing here?"

Kira flew into her arms and Lea squealed with joy. "It's a long story," she told her friend, swiping the last remnants of tears from her eyes.

Lea took one look at her and said, "Come on in. We can talk while I prepare the cabin."

"Hey Kira." For the first time, she noticed Arlo seated in the lounge, hailing her with his clipboard. Wonderful. Just who she needed to see. She hoped against hope his mission tonight was to monitor and rat on the ticket agents instead of the cabin crew. Unfortunately, she'd have no way of knowing until the doors were sealed. He had clearance to board at any time.

This royally sucked. Kira did not want him to be privy to the soap opera turn her life had taken.

"Hi Arlo," she murmured.

He got up and sauntered over. "Jack says you two are an item." He didn't mince words. "I was hoping we could work it out."

"Save it Arlo," she said. "You made your choice in Seattle."

"That was just a fling. You and I had something," he said.

How pathetic could you get? "*Had* being the operative word. You blew it big-time." And thank God. If he hadn't been such a prick, she would never have had her time with Jack, and even though it was over, at least she had the memories.

Arlo winced. "You know how flight crews are—"

"How are they, turdhead?" Lea asked, not waiting for an answer. "C'mon, sweet face." She pulled Kira through the door. Arms linked, they hurried down the jetway.

"You and Jack?" Lea hissed out of the side of her mouth, hitching carefully penciled eyebrows. "Oh boy. This is going to be good."

"Later," Kira whispered, casting a covert over-the-shoulder glance to check on Arlo. He hadn't followed.

"Gotcha," Lea said as they filed into the empty jet and assumed position.

While the rest of the various crews worked, Kira followed Lea to the rear of the plane and filled her in on the latest developments. Lea listened intently, frowning at all the proper moments then stopped to embrace Kira tightly after she'd finished the sad tale.

"I don't know what to tell you, kiddo," Lea said. "I'd bet my life he loves you, but I sure do understand your point of view."

"What am I going to do?"

"The guy wants to marry you," Lea said. Thankfully, the clanging of stainless steel as she set up the galley kept her strident voice from carrying throughout the cabin. "A few years down the road, you might get an *I love you* out of this. Assuming you let him live long enough."

"But I might not ever hear it. What then?"

Lea pressed full, glossy lips tight. "The way I see it, you have two choices. Accept him for who he is, or dump him."

Accept him for who he is. Hadn't she been doing that all along? Hadn't it been enough all these years? Wasn't it what true lovers did for each other? On the other hand, what about *her* needs? Didn't they count for anything?

"You guys go back a long way," Lea continued. "You're part of each other. Truthfully, I wouldn't know what to do with you if you didn't have Jack in your life. You'd be so altered."

"Would you still be my friend?"

"Oh honey, of course. I didn't mean that." They hugged again. "I mean you'd need more than I could give, like therapy or something, you know? Dumping Jack would be like cutting off an arm."

"Or cutting out my heart." Kira slumped into a jump seat and eyed her beautiful friend.

"You'd be dead without him," Lea said.

That she would.

She stared at the patterned upholstery on the seat back in front of her. Unfocused eyes saw the delicate sheen of expensive, sturdy fabric. When she focused, she spotted some travel-worn pilling, a few loose threads.

That was Jack's soul, she thought. Glossy on the surface, weary when you looked closer.

Was she asking too much of him?

What if he started demanding things she couldn't give? Being as demanding as her father? At first, she'd thought he was. But she'd learned differently. He hadn't changed.

She had.

Maybe it was time she grew up and realized that one person couldn't give you everything you needed. Maybe her expectations needed adjusting.

He showed her how much he cared every day, every minute. Wouldn't she rather have the actions than the words?

No. Unlike her mother, she needed the words. She *definitely* needed the words. But maybe getting those words was worth a little more effort on her part. Jack wasn't as strong as he looked. She'd just have to *make* him say it.

"I'm going to keep trying." Man, that sounded good. "I don't care if it takes a year, or if I have to beat him over the head with a stick. He's not getting off the hook that easily." Clarity of purpose propelled her to her feet.

"That's my girl." Lea winked. "Sic 'em."

Passengers had begun boarding and the cabin bustled with activity. About to thread her way through the throng, a commotion in first class froze her dead in her tracks.

Jack came striding down the aisle.

Kira's heart burst into flames at the sight of him. Even out of uniform, he had such a commanding presence once he stepped foot in a plane that he made everyone else look like drones. She plopped back down from the impact.

Down the long aisle he came, his gaze locked on hers with laser-like intensity. Passengers parted in front of him, stumbling into the seats and hitting their heads on the overhead bins to clear a path. Even Lea ducked out of sight when she saw him, and she was usually fearless in his presence, fond of her little hobby of ticking him off.

Odd. Kira noticed a slight limp in his gait and when her eyes flew to his face, she saw it looked tight and grim, as if he were in pain.

Wordlessly, he stopped in front of her, yanked her out of the seat and into his arms. Grabbing her chin in one hand, he ground out, "I love you," and covered her mouth with his before she could so much as blink.

The passion in his kiss telegraphed straight to her knees and they buckled under the weight of it. Jack caught her deftly by the waist, lips never leaving hers, and clamped her to him, bending her backwards and kissing her like there was no tomorrow.

When he finally broke free, she was gasping for breath, heart pounding like a marching band. "I love you," he announced again, voice raspy, deep and loud. "Marry me."

A rousing cheer went up through the cabin as passengers became enraptured by the scene, applauding and stomping. Kira grew dizzy from the heat in his eyes and the racing blood in her veins. The drama of his declaration left her panting and wanting and so much in love she could hardly bear it. Somehow she had to get a grip so she could examine all that had happened and make certain he meant what he said.

She knew how badly he wanted to please her father, and if this was simply one last-ditch effort to tell her what she wanted to hear so she'd marry him, forget it.

Mentally hoisting her bootstraps, she drew herself up and looked Jack straight in the eye. "You're just saying you love me because you want to fulfill Dad's wish." There. It was on the table. Jack reared back, stunned. At the same time Lea poked her head out of the galley.

"I think he means it this time, kiddo."

"Hush up!" Kira silenced her friend with a scowl. But the sibilant word carried and the entire cabin fell quiet.

"What does she know about this?" Jack pointed to Lea.

"Everything." Kira lifted her chin. "A girl needs her friends."

"Right on, sister," came a voice from the front of the plane.

Jack started the old neck roll routine but stopped himself abruptly, bringing his hand down to his pocket and extracting a small blue box. With a slight wince, he lowered to one knee, looking vulnerable and un-Jack-like. He looked up at her, blue raspberry eyes liquid and huge, and opened the box to display a dazzling flash of diamond.

"Kira," he said. "I would never marry you just because your father wanted me to. I'm here now, begging you to marry me because I love you with everything I've got. I always have and I always will and we've wasted so much damn time already. Will you please say yes?"

Acceptance was tingling on the tip of her tongue when her inner imp came out of hiding. Try though she might, she couldn't resist teasing a little.

"When did you have time to get an engagement ring?"

"Shut up and put it on."

"Looks like it came from a gumball machine."

"Tell that to my checking account."

"It probably won't fit. You always screw these things up."

His lips twitched, eyes glittering with the light of battle. "I think this time, I finally managed to get it right."

"Let's see about that." She extended her left hand.

Jack popped the ring out of the satin holder and poised it over her fingertip. As he did so he said, "For the third time, I love you. Marry me." His voice was so flat and banal she had to smile.

"Seems anticlimactic," she said, but tears filled her eyes as the slippery smooth platinum hit the end of her finger.

"I wonder why," Lea muttered and everybody laughed.

Jack stood and looked down at her, folding her hand into his and lifting it to his lips. "What do you say?" he asked softly.

After all this, he still felt unsure. Love swelled to a crescendo as she gazed at this wonderful man, her cherished friend and lover who stood by her through good times and bad, taking care of her even as he teased her mercilessly. Now, finally, he would be her husband. The warmth of that word settled around her like a well-worn blanket. Husband. Jack Grayson would be her husband.

In the hush of the cabin, she stroked his dear face. "I say yes."

Epilogue

Moral dilemma number thirteen –
Does anyone have the right to be this happy?

"Yeah. That's it, baby."

"Like this, Jack?"

"Slow and easy. Damn you're good."

"Sliding down."

"Lower. Yes! Kiss it. Oh my God. Grease it, baby. Yes!"

Kira retracted the reverser and disengaged the auto brakes as the mighty jet screamed down to taxi speed on Heathrow's runway.

"God that was good. I think I came. Did you hear me?"

"Everyone heard you, Jack. It's on the black box."

"They're applauding in the back. You're smoother than scotch." He leaned over and sucked on her lips. "So damn hot when you land."

"Bet you say that to all your copilots."

"You're the best."

"I hope so." She smiled.

"Don't doubt it." Jack taxied the plane to the terminal gate, welcomed the passengers to the United Kingdom and finished shut-down procedure while the plane emptied out.

"I want to make an addendum to the deal." He stood, flipped the clasp on Tom's cockpit case—her wedding gift to him—and set it reverently on his seat.

"A year later and you're changing the deal? No can do," Kira answered crisply. She quickly filled out a gripe sheet to leave in the cockpit for the mechanics and took one last glug of coffee.

"I let you make addendums," he complained.

She rolled her eyes at him. "No you don't. You twist them around to suit your needs and try to make me believe I'm getting away with something."

"Busted." Jack laughed. "I can never keep ahead of my wife."

And Lord knew he tried. Constantly. This past year, it seemed his reason for living had become to pull one over on her.

"That's right. So don't bother trying. Addendum denied."

"Hear me out."

She sighed, straightening from her papers and smoothing her hair. "Shoot."

He gazed at her, a curious light in his eye. A rare and bright English sun streamed into the cockpit. "Right here on the flight deck, where it all started, I want it to end."

What on earth?

He continued. "We can't fly together anymore."

Though his face looked grave, she heard a tease in his voice. "And why is that?" Another trick. She had to be on her toes all the time.

He drew a deep breath. "We would be in violation of Pan Air Safety Code."

"Been drinking beer with Arlo again?" It was a joke between them, whenever Jack got his dander up about her supposed recklessness. Which was still too often. But getting better every day. "Want to speak English?"

He pulled her close, nuzzling her hair. A fingertip at her chin tilted her face up and he kissed her reverently. "Pan Air doesn't allow married couples with children to pilot the same plane."

"I know."

He pulled back an inch. "Do I have to spell it out for you?"

"In a word. Yes." She had an inkling what he meant, but torturing him was still too much fun. She could still get him worked up if she tried hard enough, or took him by surprise. But it was getting more and more difficult to yank his chain.

Jack groaned and pushed her gently away. He ducked his head with uncharacteristic shyness, and a hand crept up to massage his neck. "I want to have a baby."

He wanted a child with her. Jack. Who once believed his only choice in life was to stay unattached. The man who once ran hell-for-leather from emotion, wanted a baby. A soft, warm sigh escaped her lips and he lifted his face to bask in it.

She moved closer. "Once again, you're late on the draw, Grayson." Love clogged her throat and made her voice husky. She shook her head and smoothed his stubbly cheeks with her hands.

"What's that supposed to mean?" His lean body curled against hers, hard, hot and ready for action. But also curiously vulnerable.

"I was going to tell you later. In a more romantic setting—" she whispered.

"What could be more romantic than this?"

She had to agree. This past year, flying with Jack in jets and lying with Jack on layovers across the world, had quite simply been the most exhilarating time in her life. There wasn't an experience known to mankind that could top it.

Except maybe one.

"What could be more romantic?" she reiterated. "How about you and me wanting a baby at the same time, and getting one."

His voice cracked. "Are you telling me we have one already?"

She pressed herself tightly into his arms. Her best friend, her husband and now the father of her child.

"Yeah. That's what I'm telling you."

"So I finally got my addendum."

"And a free gift for opening this account." She smiled.

He closed his eyes and swayed against her. "We're both going to raise our child. Together."

She nodded against the solid warmth of his chest. "You and me, Jack. Together. Always."

Enjoy this excerpt from

Summer in the City of Sails

"I want you to look after Summer."

Summer's bare feet froze outside the door to her Uncle Henry's study. Her hand slid from the brass doorknob. A babysitter? Indignation stabbed her mind, robbing her of the sense of accomplishment she'd felt only seconds earlier. At age twenty-two, why did they think she needed a babysitter? Her eyes narrowed as she placed the package she carried on a wooden pedestal table then pressed closer to hear the details.

"Do I look like a babysitter?" a masculine voice snapped. "Try the yellow pages."

Summer nodded emphatically, giving a silent cheer for the owner of the low, husky voice. *Way to go, mister.* But while she waited for Uncle Henry's comeback, she fumed. She knew exactly where the idea had originated. Her family. Or more specifically her mother who thought danger lurked behind every corner in sinful Auckland City.

"Think of it as a favor," Uncle Henry said.

"No."

The blunt, uncompromising answer made a smile surface. She liked this man. And she agreed with him. One hundred percent. Yes, she'd been a sickly child, but she'd outgrown the bad asthma attacks. As long as she used her inhaler, there was nothing wrong with her health. Summer glanced down at her bust and hips, her expression turning rueful. Thanks to her mother's excellent cooking, her body—well, the polite word was curvaceous.

"Nikolai," Uncle Henry groaned. "My sister will make my life miserable. She'll hunt me down on my honeymoon."

Summer suppressed a snort as she flipped the end of her French braid over her shoulder. Why did Uncle Henry think she'd come to Auckland, the city of sails? Although her mother meant well, she was overprotective, especially when it came to the baby of the family. And now she was doing the smothering thing by remote control, all the way from Eketahuna. If Summer allowed this, her bid for freedom would end before it started. It was time her family let her make her own mistakes and let her fix any stuff-ups by herself.

When her boss at the Eketahuna Library had suggested further training in big, bad Auckland City, the possibilities had made Summer breathless. Eager. At last, a chance to spread her fledgling wings. Despite her parents' protests, Summer had grasped the opportunity with both hands.

And she wasn't about to let anyone take the experience away from her.

"Tell someone who cares," Nikolai said. "With my track record, I'm the last person you should ask."

A shiver goose stepped down Summer's spine. That voice... His voice did things to her. She thought about easing the door open a little further to check out the body that matched the sexy rumble. Meeting men was high on her to-do list. No time like the present.

"I didn't want to do this," Uncle Henry muttered. "But I'm a desperate man. *You owe me*. That time I saved you from the broad in—"

The heartfelt Anglo-Saxon curse made Summer's brows shoot toward her hairline. She hadn't heard her brothers use that one before.

"All right, dammit! I'll check on her now and then, but if I see one girly tear, I'm outta there. And our debt is square once you get back."

"That should do it," Uncle Henry hastily agreed. "Just check to make sure her car is there and get a visual every couple of days."

Get a visual? Summer thought, puckering her forehead. Good grief. Nikolai was one of Uncle Henry's military friends. He'd take his duties seriously. This was not good.

"All I want is a peaceful honeymoon."

"All you want is to get laid," Nikolai muttered.

Uncle Henry chuckled—a smug masculine sound that made Summer ache to deck him on Veronica's behalf. "Yeah, that too."

Right, that did it. If she allowed this, she'd never escape her family's well-meaning influence. Yeah, she loved them, knew they loved her in return, but enough was enough.

Summer shoved the door open and strode through. "I'm back. Oh—" She stopped in front of her uncle's large wooden desk. Her hand fluttered to her left breast. "I didn't know you had a visitor."

"Summer, this is Nikolai Tarei. He's my closest neighbor."

Summer's gaze had already snapped to the man with the sexy voice. Physical awareness floored her, made her tongue stick to the roof of her mouth. Luckily, her brain continued to function and nothing impaired her twenty-twenty vision. Oh, boy! Tall, dark and sinfully sexy was welcome to guard her body *any* time.

Her uncle stood and rounded the desk to stand at her side. "Nikolai, my niece Summer. She's up in Auckland to do a six-month course at Central Library."

Nikolai shoved away from the wall and stepped across the faded blue carpet. "Pleased to meet you," he said, holding out his hand in greeting.

Summer realized her mouth gaped and snapped it shut. She stuck out her hand, and instantly it was engulfed in his warm grasp. Her heart tap-danced, did a jig—the whole works. She fought the urge to jerk her hand away. One thing stood out in her mind. This wasn't the right man to practice *Miranda's Tips to Flirting* on.

He finally released her hand and stepped back. Summer's avid gaze followed as if attached by an umbilical cord. Big. Actually, make that huge. He towered over her by a good six inches. Broad shoulders gave his black T-shirt quite a workout. Summer took in his shoulder-length unfettered hair, the stubble shading his jaw. Under no circumstances would she call him tame. Dark eyes that reminded her of the richest, most expensive chocolate skimmed her face, her body, then settled back on her uncle.

Stupidly, Summer felt the sting of rejection, but she told herself it didn't matter. Nikolai Tarei reminded her of her two brothers—extremely capable and over-protective. And one look told her it was likely he bore the bossy gene. She didn't need another brother-figure looking over her shoulder, vetting boyfriends, putting a dampener on her quest for independence. Not when she intended to let loose and live a little.

"I wanted you to meet Nikolai before I left. If you have any problems you can call on him," Uncle Henry said. His cheerful, gruff voice made Summer stiffen. Trying too hard. Did they think she was stupid?

"Most people would call that babysitting," she said, baring her teeth in a smile. Summer intercepted the brief glance the two men exchanged, the quirk of brow, the silent grimace that said, "You deal with her".

Oh, for goodness sake! "I'm not expecting any problems," she said. "I'll be too busy." She paused a beat. "Going out on the town."

Uncle Henry spluttered. His mouth opened and closed several times.

"I have to go. I'm expecting a call," Nikolai said.

Summer choked back a laugh. In military terms that qualified as a strategic retreat. Wise man. She watched him saunter to the door and frowned. What should have been a loose-limbed stride had a distinct hitch, but his black jeans covered any evidence of the injury.

"Coward," Uncle Henry muttered.

About the author:

They say there are eight million stories in the Naked City, and I think Jaci Burton wrote every single one of them. I don't know. She must've sneezed and missed a deadline because here I am at Ellora's Cave, and I couldn't be more thrilled.

Addicted to love? You bet. As well as all its sensual side effects. Great sex comes in many packages and I prefer mine wrapped in laughter, irony and sweet, edible substances. When not writing at the computer, I can be found in a fencing salle, cruising Internet auctions for vintage airline memorabilia, yelling at my children to let mommy write, or working my schleppy nine-to-fiver. When I grow up, I'd like to be a full time Ellora's Cave writer, but until then, I'll just frolic in the outskirts of the Naked City.

Bon Voyage!

Ann welcomes mail from readers. You can write to her c/o Ellora's Cave Publishing at 1056 Home Avenue, Akron OH 44310-3502.

Why an electronic book?

We live in the Information Age—an exciting time in the history of human civilization in which technology rules supreme and continues to progress in leaps and bounds every minute of every hour of every day. For a multitude of reasons, more and more avid literary fans are opting to purchase e-books instead of paperbacks. The question to those not yet initiated to the world of electronic reading is simply: *why?*

1. *Price.* An electronic title at Ellora's Cave Publishing and Cerridwen Press runs anywhere from 40-75% less than the cover price of the exact same title in paperback format. Why? Cold mathematics. It is less expensive to publish an e-book than it is to publish a paperback, so the savings are passed along to the consumer.
2. *Space.* Running out of room to house your paperback books? That is one worry you will never have with electronic novels. For a low one-time cost, you can purchase a handheld computer designed specifically for e-reading purposes. Many e-readers are larger than the average handheld, giving you plenty of screen room. Better yet, hundreds of titles can be stored within your new library—a single microchip. (Please note that Ellora's Cave and Cerridwen Press does not endorse any specific brands. You can check our website at www.ellorascave.com or

www.cerridwenpress.com for customer recommendations we make available to new consumers.)

3. *Mobility*. Because your new library now consists of only a microchip, your entire cache of books can be taken with you wherever you go.
4. *Personal preferences are accounted for*. Are the words you are currently reading too small? Too large? Too...**ANNOYING**? Paperback books cannot be modified according to personal preferences, but e-books can.
5. *Instant gratification*. Is it the middle of the night and all the bookstores are closed? Are you tired of waiting days—sometimes weeks—for online and offline bookstores to ship the novels you bought? Ellora's Cave Publishing sells instantaneous downloads 24 hours a day, 7 days a week, 365 days a year. Our e-book delivery system is 100% automated, meaning your order is filled as soon as you pay for it.

Those are a few of the top reasons why electronic novels are displacing paperbacks for many an avid reader. As always, Ellora's Cave and Cerridwen Press welcomes your questions and comments. We invite you to email us at service@ellorascave.com, service@cerridwenpress.com or write to us directly at: 1056 Home Ave. Akron OH 44310-3502.

Cerridwen, the Celtic Goddess of wisdom, was the muse who brought inspiration to storytellers and those in the creative arts. Cerridwen Press encompasses the best and most innovative stories in all genres of today's fiction. Visit our site and discover the newest titles by talented authors who still get inspired - much like the ancient storytellers did, once upon a time.

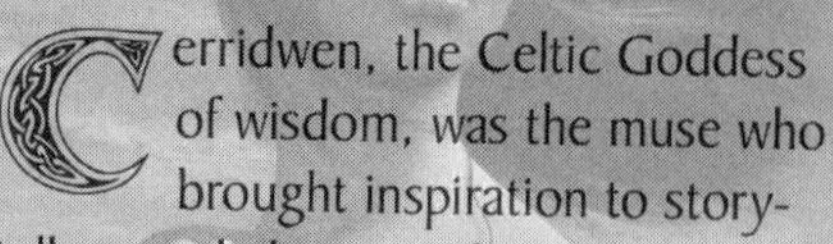